The Humundo Sorterrum

To Izz

Be Yourself

By Daniel Thompson
Illustrated by Connor Edwards

CCM BOOKS

First Published by Carefully Crafted Media in
2019
Copyright ©Daniel Thompson 2019
All Rights Reserved

Isbn - 978-1-9998295-2-0

For my wife, Sophie.

With special thanks to all those who supported this book.

Did you ever stop to wonder,
How you came to be that shape?
Are you moulded out of plasticine,
Or held with sellotape?

Is there string upon your fingers,
That moves them as they do?
Is your hair sewn in with cotton,
Or just stuck up there with glue?

Are there hinges in your elbows?
Are there hinges in your knees?
Are your toes in fact 10 soldiers,
Who were told to stand at ease?

Well if you have been asking,
All those questions in your head.
I suspect you'll be delighted,
With the pages up ahead.

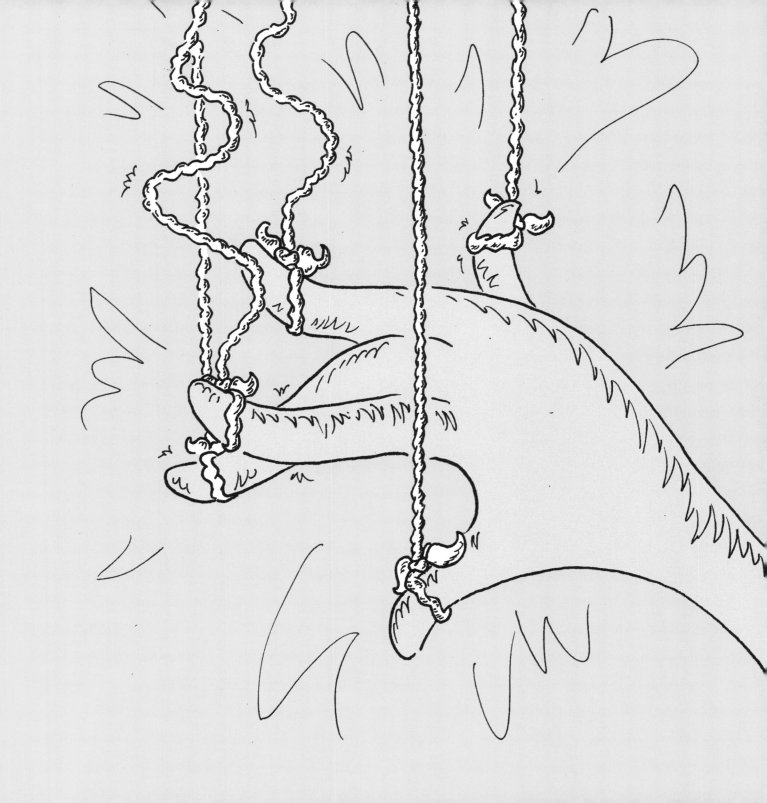

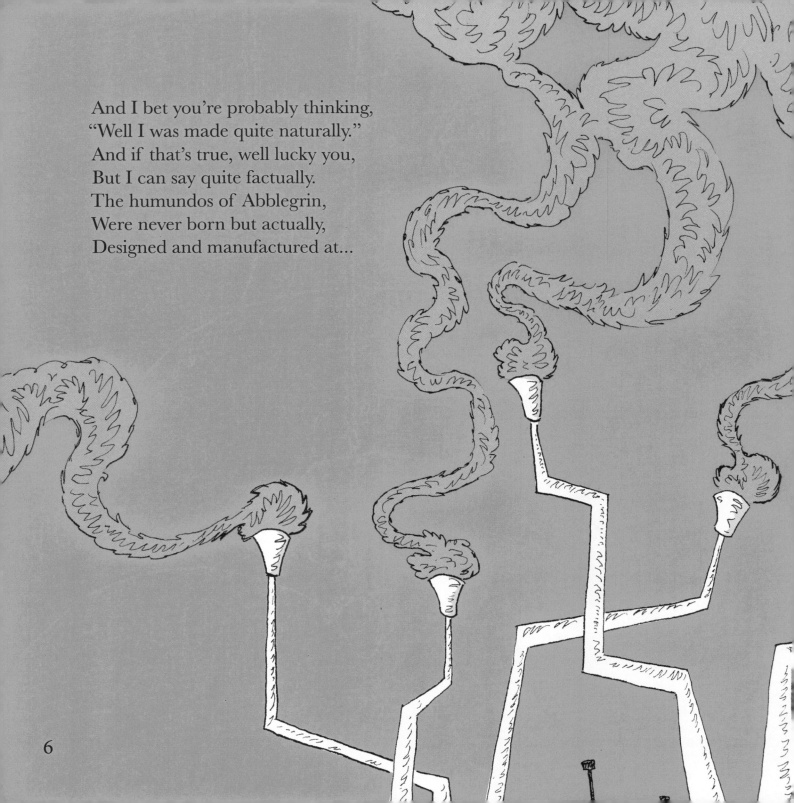

And I bet you're probably thinking,
"Well I was made quite naturally."
And if that's true, well lucky you,
But I can say quite factually.
The humundos of Abblegrin,
Were never born but actually,
Designed and manufactured at...

The **Humundo Sorterium** baby making factory...

At the edge of Abblegrin,
Beneath a blackened cloud.
Lies a place where all have been,
But no one is allowed.

A hundred dirty windows,
Piled several stories high.
Three half-collapsed old chimney stacks,
Cough smoke into the sky.

A place described by Grandpa,
Who snuck in as a lad.
As a factory, spectacularly,
Despicably bad.

"Can it really be that awful?"
Said Buddy somewhat miffed.
"I heard it's where humundos go,
To collect their baby gift."

"Their baby gift?" Said Grandpa,
"Is that what they're saying now?
Well it is where babies come from…
But did they ever tell you how?

Back when I was just a boy,
You'd see storks flying in.
As they carried new humundos,
'Cross the skies of Abblegrin.

Back then they came from nature,
Each baby was unique.
With different eyes and different cries,
And different hands and feet.

Now initially, that factory,
Was made to help the storks.
The Humundo Sorterium,
Reduced the hours they worked.

But as the years went on and on,
The storks flew less and less.
'Till eventually they didn't really,
Need to leave their nests.

Beneath those factory chimneys,
Behind those factory walls,
The Humundo Sorterium,
Took over from them all.

Then one wicked winter,
After several years of loss.
Baroness Von Adlevine,
Took over as the boss.

"In zee interest of proficiency,
To increase zee population.
Zhis factory's efficiency,
Is under observation.

Zee problem is..." said Adlevine,
"Each baby is unique.
With different eyes and different cries,
And different hands and feet."

And so it was decided,
To reduce the workers' salaries.
And to make humundo babies,
With less individualities.

More babies made,
More body parts.
More matching bones,
More matching hearts.

More matching brains,
More all-the-sames.
Less room for thoughts,
Less fun and games."

While Buddy sat and listened,
To the words his Grandpa said.
He couldn't stop his wonderer,
From wandering round his head.

14

Was it really possible?
Do humundos make such blunders?
I mean, it seems important,
All humundos should be wonders!

It wasn't he didn't believe him,
It's just sometimes when asked,
Grandpa could exaggerate,
These stories from his past.

So Buddy had decided,
The best thing he could do,
Was take a walk to find a stork,
And ask if it was true.

So Buddy packed jam sandwiches,
And a piece of chocolate cake.
And once his Grandpa fell asleep,
He headed for the lake.

It took him half an hour or so,
To walk through Abblegrin.
He passed the local village pub,
With all the locals in.

He passed the local bus stop,
He passed the local store.
He passed a rotting carrot,
In a puddle on the floor.

He walked across a field,
And underneath the wood.
He tip-toed through the river,
'Till his socks were full of mud.

And then at last before him,
He saw as he'd been told.
A mustering of mighty storks,
Around a watering hole.

"Excuse me sir," said Buddy,
To the first stork he could see.
"I'm after information,
On the baby factory?"

That stork he huffed, his feathers puffed,
He looked a real scruff muffin.
"Us storks we don't remember much,
And I's remember nothin'.

I's afraid I's lost my brains,
But speak to Handsome Henry.
He's known throughout this watering hole,
For his photo-magraphic memory."

And then all of a sudden,
From high above the crowds.
A face somewhat familiar,
Came soaring through the clouds.

His wing span was magnificent,
His hair was neatly kept.
This stork looked very different,
From the others he had met.

Was this Handsome Henry?
Buddy could have sworn,
Although he didn't know him,
That he'd seen his face before.

"Excuse me sir, but have we met?"
Buddy began to talk.
"It's just I feel I know you,
But I've never met a stork?"

"I knows exactly who you isn't,"
Handsome Henry said.
"I was him what brought you,
To your birthing baby bed.

I thoughts I was mistaken,
But now I sees it's Buddy.
You is far much bigger now,
And your feets is far more muddy."

As he spoke, his voice it choked,
His eyes they filled with misery.
"I's recognise you anywhere,
Yous was my last delivery.

In fact you is the last born son,
To be put together naturally.
Before that barmpot Baroness,
Took over in that factory."

Buddy's wonderer halted,
In a state of flabbergast.
Although absurd, his Grandpa's words,
Were nailed onto the mast.

Then all at once his wonderer,
It started twice as fast.
With a myriad of questions,
That he hadn't thought to ask.

"Who is this Von Adlevine?
What's a Baroness?
So do they use a factory line?
Or hatch them in a nest?

Where even is this factory?
Is it nearby?"
He rattled off a couple more,
Then stopped for a reply.

A vacant blank expression,
Filled Handsome Henry's face.
"You's askin' all those questions,
Like they's in a running race.

Now I's would likes to helps you,
I really truly would.
Buts the Humundo Sorterium,
Has never been no good.

They's rows and rows of boxes,
Piled upon a shelf.
They makes just 9 humundos,
And absolutely nothing else.

One for tall and one for small,
And ones for thin and fat.
Ones for bones, and ones for tones,
That comes in white or black.

They's one for girls and one for boys,
And the last one at the back.
Is a scruffy looking broken box,
What's labelled 'this and that'.

They's never mix them boxes,
They's always stay the same.
Same nose, same toes,
Same hair what grows,
Same teeny tiny brains."

Buddy interrupted,
His wonderer in a spin.
"Let's mix up all the body parts,
And the boxes that they're in.

Then all the new humundos,
Born from that day on.
Would be uniquely wonderful,
They'd be the only one."

"That's the ways it used to be,"
  Handsome Henry said.
"Before that evil Adlevine,
  Got all us storks misled."

"Then take me to the factory,
  Let's stop this heinous crime."
But Handsome Henry stuttered,
  "I've not been there in some time.

My brain's a whirling fliperty jib,
  Full of whizzers and fizzers and pops.
For every thought it's kept inside,
  There's five that it's forgot.

But if I close my eyes a while,
And thinks back really well.
I sees it in my mind a bit,
But not enough to tell.

I sees beneath a blackened cloud,
A field where nothing grows.
And the only flappers flapping round,
Bes crooked clockwork crows.

I sees big gates of iron,
And smoke up in the sky.
I see that daft old statue,
We was always flying by."

"Ooooh!" Bumped Buddy's wonderer,
"What statue do you see?
'Cause there's a big old statue,
In the town not far from me."

"His name be Edgar Abblegrin?"
Said Henry peering down.
"Yes!" Said Buddy, "I know it well,
He's the founder of our town."

"Hmph," said Henry huffing,
"Well that I's do not know.
But if you know where Edgar is,
Then maybe we can go."

"I do! I do!" Shrieked Buddy,
"But it's really quite a walk."
"Walk?" Said Handsome Henry,
"I's think not, I's a stork.

Wrap yourself in swaddle cloth,
From head down to your feet.
Now tie it up into a knot,
And place it in my beak."

Henry called the other storks,
To help him get them set.
They preened his mighty feathers,
Just in case of getting wet.

They formed a mighty runway,
All aglow with fireflies.
Then Handsome Henry took a run,
And leaped into the skies.

Now Buddy had once took a trip,
On a tin can aeroplane.
He hadn't liked it much at all,
But this was not the same.

This feeling was magnificent,
Exciting yet serene.
He peered down at the world below,
And saw where he had been.

He saw the muddy river,
Beneath him as he flew.
He saw the tiny people,
Passing by and pushing through.

He saw the village local,
He saw the village shop.
He saw his own front garden,
And his rooftop chimney pot.

Buddy called directions,
And led them down a street.
Until that old stone statue,
Came to stand beneath their feet.

"That's the boy," said Henry,
"I knows the way from him.
It's left, then right, then left, left right,
Then loop-de-loop and spin."

"Are you really certain?"
Buddy said out loud.
But before he got an answer back,
He saw that blackened cloud.

He saw the field of furrows,
Where nothing grew at all.
He saw those crooked chimney stacks,
A hundred meters tall.

But then all of a flurry,
They came under attack.
One thousand tiny fighter planes,
All dressed in suits of black.

"It's them crooked clockwork crows,
They's always on her land.
I's can't fly a mile more,
I's gonna have to land."

And so the two crash landed,
Into a field of dirt.
Buddy bounced a little bit,
But nobody was hurt.

He dusted down his trousers,
And he lifted up his eyes.
To which he saw a MURDER…
…Of crows amongst the skies.

Down they came around him,
Dive-bombing in their rows.
Four and twenty jet black birds,
All set to peck his nose.

Buddy's wonderer panicked,
He knew not what to do.
He shut his eyes and waited,
For the moment to be through.

But once amongst the darkness,
He soon began to see.
"One hundred crows around my head,
But none are pecking me."

So each eye slowly opened,
And there before his toes.
A bird as black as night itself,
Stood proud amongst the crows.

This bird was somewhat larger,
The same, yet something else.
Then Buddy had a memory,
Of a book upon his shelf.

"The crow" he recollected,
"Is a family relation.
To the larger Corvus Corax,
A.K.A the common raven."

"Hello, I'm Madame Megan,
Please excuse this animosity.
But it's my duty to inform you,
That you've entered private property."

"We've come to stop Von Adlevine."
Said Buddy unperturbed.
"And no one's going to stop us,
Not you or any birds."

"I'm sorry if this comes to you,
As bitter disappointment.
But Baroness Von Adlevine,
Meets only by appointment."

Buddy was dumbfounded,
He felt so out of place.
But just as he was giving in,
That raven changed her face.

She beckoned Buddy closer,
And whispered in his ear.
"The birds you see before you,
They are not as they appear.

Each crow is made mechanically,
Designed as fighter spies.
Their beaks have built in microphones,
There's cameras in their eyes.

They form a tiny army,
To serve and to protect.
Programmed to report back,
All suspicions they suspect.

Now I'd really like to help you,
As I'm here against my will.
But if I say just one thing wrong,
These crows are trained to kill.

There used to be more ravens,
But as the years went on.
They disobeyed the Baroness,
Now all of them are gone!"

Buddy's wonderer wobbled,
As he tried to think it through.
"But we need to stop Von Adlevine,
Is there nothing we can do?"

Megan took a second,
To assess her situation.
She checked no crows were listening,
Then she shared some information.

"Well... there is one rumour,
Of a worker discontented,
Who programmed in a secret code,
When the crows were first invented.

It's said a certain trigger word,
Can activate that code.
And if that word is said aloud,
Their heads will all explode."

"The problem is," said Megan,
"To hide his secret weapon.
He set the magic trigger word,
As the answer to a question.

Now I can ask that riddle,
I know the way it goes.
But what that trigger code word is,
Is something no one knows.

But if you were to say it,
And if the rumour's true.
All the crows will self-destruct,
And you could walk right through."

With that she hopped three paces back,
Then forward just a little.
"If our path you wish to pass,
You first must solve this riddle.

The rules are very simple,
Listen to my rhyme.
Think about it… talk about it…
Take a little time.

I'll even give three chances,
For you to make your guess.
But should you get three answers wrong…
You'll be placed under arrest.

The Baroness Von Adlevine,
Will decide your final fate.
And I am not to speak for her,
But I assure you… it won't be great.

So my dears, the choice is yours,
Do you dare to play?
Or will you use your common sense,
To turn and walk away?"

Henry's feathers quivered,
He'd shrunk down somewhat small.
It seemed to be quite clear,
He didn't want to play at all.

But Buddy loved a riddle,
He did them with his Ma.
And he couldn't bear to turn around,
Not now they'd come so far.

"Ask it!" Shouted Buddy,
"I have to make things right."
Henry interrupted,
"Now I's not one to fright.

But I's did not agree to that!"
His words he blurted fast.
But Henry knew that riddle,
Was already being asked.

The crowd of crows fell silent,
Megan cleared her throat.
"May your brains be with you..."
And then these words she spoke.

"I'll show you lakes, but you can't swim,
I'm filled with towns with nothing in.
I harbor forests, but never trees,
There are no fish beneath my seas.
I'm miles thin from sea to sky,
I am you all, but what am I?"

Buddy's wonderer whistled,
Henry looked perplexed.
"I's never heard of anything
So wobbly and complex."

They stood 300 seconds,
Each furrowed on his brow.
"No trees inside a forest?
It must be true, but how?"

"I know it!" Shouted Buddy,
"It's a case of misdirection.
All those things are what you see,
When you look in a reflection.

Towns with no one in them,
Seas without the fish.
Lakes that you can't swim in,
Oh I'm sure it must be this!"

Henry was astounded,
He showered him in praise.
"What a clever answer,
It works in all those ways."

Megan shrugged her shoulders,
"A noble guess indeed.
But I see no heads exploding,
So it's not the one I need."

"Rats!" Said Handsome Henry,
"My brain is flabbergasting.
Instead of finding answers,
I's found questions to be asking."

"Oh maybe," Buddy bundled,
His confidence elated.
"You could find those kinds of things,
In a picture that's been painted."

So Buddy shouted… "PAINTING!"
Without another thought.
Megan took a look around,
Then back came her retort.

"A truly stunning answer,
A tough one to reject.
But with so many heads intact,
It seems you're incorrect."

"Double rats!" Cried Henry,
"I've not a diddly-do.
We's only gets three guesses,
And that guess was number two."

He huffled and he puffled,
He searched his brains and back.
"I's couldn't find your answer,
If you's showed me on a map."

"Say that again," said Buddy,
Henry looked perplexed.
"I's was only saying,
That we's on our final guess."

"No, not that!" Said Buddy,
His wonderer in a flap.
"You said you couldn't find it,
If she showed you on a map."

"Well maybe," muttered Henry,
"Either that or somethin' else.
But I's not exactly certain,
How's you think that's going to help."

"A map!" Said Buddy bursting,
"Oh Henry! Don't you see?
A map can have a forest,
But can never have a tree.

A map has lakes and oceans,
And a map is full of towns.
But it doesn't have a single,
Living creature walking 'round."

"I's said that?" Said Henry,
He sounded quite unsure.
"I mean… I said that!"
He tried again, more certain than before.

"I knew that I'd had known it,
Once all my brains aligned."
Buddy knew he hadn't,
But he let him have his pride.

"It's got to be, it has to be,
If not, I'll eat my hat."
He turned to Madame Megan,
"I would like to answer MAP!"

Megan stood stone silent,
Had they got it wrong?
Then somewhat unexpectedly,
The crows burst into song.

A chorus line erupted,
They sang in harmony.
"The one to solve the riddle,
Is the one to set us free."

One crow flew up skyward,
In a way somewhat berserk.
And with a blast exploded,
Like a raging firework.

A dozen more went skyward,
They whistled as they flew.
Kaboom! Shabang! Kafizzle! Pop!
Bright blazes as they blew.

Before another moment,
Had the time to slip away.
A hundred more went skywards,
In a firework display.

Buddy stood astounded,
Until the final crow,
Shuttled through the atmosphere,
And set the skies aglow.

"You did it!" Shouted Megan,
She held to Henry tight.
"You saved me from my captors,
What skill! What wit! What might!"

Poor Handsome Henry blushelled,
'Till now he'd never been,
Someone else's hero,
Except once inside a dream.

But before he got to relish,
In his first heroic act.
Buddy tugged his feathers,
And reality was back.

"Okay Henry, this is it,
We're at the factory gates.
The Humundo Sorterium,
Is somewhere in that place.

Let's go!" He said ecstatically,
Goose tingles on his skin.
"Ooh Megan, tell us, do you know,
A way we could sneak in?"

Megan flapped her feathers,
And set herself to soar.
"They keep an open window,
Furthest left, above the door."

She looked to Handsome Henry,
"You really are a wise one."
Then up she flew and disappeared,
Somewhere on the horizon.

They turned to face the factory,
Henry full of pride.
"As I is a real life hero,
I's will get us both inside."

With Buddy on his shoulders,
And his attitude refractory.
He flew right through that window,
Landing deep inside the factory.

"Bravo! Bravo!" Called Buddy,
"We made it, look around."
"Well I's am a real life hero,
I's'll never let you down."

The Sorterium

Buddy's wonderer puzzled,
"How are we going to find,
The Humundo Sorterium?
...Oh look there's a sign.

That way to the offices,
And left to the aquarium.
Oh look, look there, it says it there,
The Humundo Sorterium.

66

It says it's this direction,
It says it's on this floor.
And I'll bet my boots it's written,
On the outside of its door."

So quietly they tiptoed,
Down darkened dreary halls.
And shushed at their own shadows,
As they crept along the walls.

Soon they found a doorway,
To a quite humongous room.
Where the cobwebs in it's corners,
Tried to warn you of its gloom.

It's every skylight filthy,
It's windows all the same.
There hung a dusty picture,
In a dusty picture frame.

The lights were low and heavy,
The air was full of dust.
It smelt of rotting nettles,
As the metals turned to rust.

But stood still in the centre,
Just as Grandpa had said.
The Humundo Sorterium,
Fired full steam ahead.

Smoke puffed from its puffers,
Oil dripped from its drippers.
A spinner spun a tiny thumb,
Then dipped it in it's dippers.

Dials were dealing digits,
There were buttons by the score.
A thousand knobs and levers,
From the top down to the floor.

A network of conveyor belts,
With all their wheels wheeling.
Were ferrying small body parts,
To the tip top of the ceiling.

They dropped them into funnels,
That fed this huge machine.
It really was the strangest thing,
The two had even seen.

And right down at the bottom,
As Henry had described.
Nine gigantic boxes,
Overflowing with supplies.

"This whole thing is ridiculous."
Buddy said out loud.
"It couldn't be, it wouldn't be,
It shouldn't be allowed.

This whole thing makes me angry,
From my nose down to my socks.
You can't build all humundos,
From a dirty cardboard box.

Quick Henry, press some buttons,
Let's see what this thing's got.
If we can overload it,
Then production has to stop."

Buddy pulled a lever,
He pushed some buttons in.
A siren started sounding,
And the dials began to spin.

He looked around to Henry,
Who'd barely moved a feather.
And written clear across his face,
The tell tale signs of terror.

"What's wrong with you?" Said Buddy.
But he didn't move a bone.
Then Buddy got the feeling,
That the two were not alone.

He tried to calm his wonderer,
As it spiraled into stress.
He knew deep down it had to be,
The fabled Baroness.

He slowly turned to face her,
His heart beat double time.
There before his very eyes,
He saw Von Adlevine.

She towered high above him,
Square shouldered and rotund.
He thought he might be braver,
But he couldn't find his tongue.

"What do you think you're doing boy?"
She bellowed in his face.
"You really shouldn't meddle,
In another person's place."

"We've come to put a stop to you,
His tongue returned to say.
You can't make all humundos,
In this idiotic way.

There should be no labels,
No tones or measured heights.
No noted personalities,
No moulds of any type.

Each child should have a fingerprint,
Not only on their thumb.
But a fingerprint of who they are,
And who they will become."

"Oh is zhat so?" Said Adlevine,
"And you think I've met my ruin?
At ze hands of such a tiny child,
With no clue for what he's doing?"

"It's not just me!" Said Buddy,
"Henry's here as well.
And he's a real life hero,
Who will send you straight to hell."

But as he looked to Henry,
To bolster his attack.
It seemed that hero Henry,
Had just turned his hero back.

It was a real humdingerling,
An unwelcome surprise.
"Oh dear! I zink your hero,
Has just left you here to die!

I've never recalled a product,
But you can be ze first.
I'll put you in ze finished pile,
Zhen set it to reverse.

First it pulls your fingers off,
And zhen your smelly toes.
Zhen it disconnects your legs,
And takes your earlobes.

Next it pulls your arms off,
And finally, your head.
And instead of being a nosy boy,
You'll just be a nose instead."

She took a step towards him,
Buddy backed away.
But corned by the cobwebs,
There was nothing more to say.

He closed his eyes and waited,
For the moment to be through.
He hadn't planned this part at all,
He knew not what to do.

Then all upon a wallop,
There came a brouhaha.
A flood of light, a smash of glass,
Commotion from afar.

Buddy's one eye opened,
And in a flash he caught,
A glimpse of Handsome Henry,
And a hundred other storks.

They tumbled through the windows,
The light came flooding back.
All around the Baroness,
They dived and pecked and scratched.

78

79

She flapped her arms to fend them off,
She stumbled back and forth.
But she couldn't get her bearings,
Underneath the diving storks.

Henry swooped upon her,
She tripped on her shoelaces.
And fell in to the finished box,
In a way somewhat ungracious.

80

Buddy started pressing,
Every button he could find.
'Til the Humundo Sorterium,
Switched over to rewind.

The Baroness, she disappeared,
Back into the machine…
And I'm not going to lie to you,
They heard her wail and scream.

The dials they span a double,
The wonky pipes they wobbled.
The Baroness Von Adlevine,
Was well and truly gobbled.

Then all the spinning spinners,
And the puffing puffers stopped.
The whistlers didn't whistle,
And the poppers didn't pop.

Buddy's wonderer settled,
The storks began to land.
He ran right up to Henry,
And he grabbed him by the hand.

"Thank you, thank you Henry!
I thought you'd flew away."
"No… I's only left a minute,
So's that I could save the day."

"We did it!" Shouted Buddy,
"We did it! You and me!
 Now every new humundo born,
 Will be who they will be."

"The problem is," said Henry,
"I's quite unsure exactly,
 How's you thinks it will be working,
 Now that we control the factory?"

Buddy started smiling,
"Henry, don't be cross.
 But I thought you might take over,
 As the factory's new boss."

"Who, me?" Said Henry startled,
 His face a shade of white.
"Yes! This factory needs a hero,
 That can bring it back to life."

"Well I suppose," said Henry,
"I could take this factory.
 And mix up the machinery,
 With the humundos born naturally."

"Not could but should!" Said Buddy,
 So they started on that day.
 Three weeks passed, they'd cleared the glass,
 And threw each box away.

The factory re-opened,
A stork in every role.
With every new humundo,
Made in individual moulds.

Henry welcomed Buddy,
"Come look what we've achieved.
We's taken bits from nature,
Like their hopes and fears and dreams.

We's mixed them with the new ways,
Re-programmed the machine.
And once we's got the balance right,
Theys made the perfect team.

So from now on all babies born,
And grown in Abblegrin,
Will be uniquely wonderfuls,
Both outside and within!"

Buddy's wonderer dazzled,
At the feat that he'd achieved.
All because he stood up for,
The things that he believed.

And from that day to this one,
It's absolutely true.
Humundos born on planet Earth,
From me right back to you.

Are made entirely wonderful,
And long may it remain.
For wouldn't it be boring,
If we all were born the same.

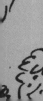

So that's the story over,
Which leaves me just to say.
Whoever you are, whatever you are,
Well that's perfectly okay.

But should you feel different,
Here's a secret barely known.
The most amazing people,
Are the ones who stand alone.

So always look for sunshine,
Even when the clouds are black.
Someday soon the wind will blow,
And bring the blue skies back.

THE END

I'm Danny; a poet, film maker, musician and all round creative human from Birmingham.

I've long felt that (now more than ever) there is a lot of social pressure on us all to 'fit the mould' rather than express ourselves on an individual level.

I have written this book to say that the best way to be interesting is to be yourself and do things your own way. You are the only one of you and that should be celebrated. Well done you!

Thank you for reading my book, I hope you enjoyed it.

I'm Connor, an illustrator from Birmingham. We have worked together on both 'The Christmas Tale of Elaine Gale' and 'The Humundo Sorterium'.

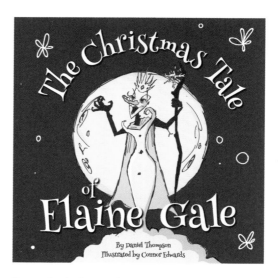

You can also check out Dan's first title, 'The Christmas Tale of Elaine Gale'

THE AUSTRALIAN
Women's Weekly

GRATINS & BAKES
PASTA • VEGTABLES • POTATOES • FISH • CHICKEN • MEAT

acp
books

contents

Pasta 4

Vegetables 24

Potatoes 40

Seafood 52

Chicken 72

Meat 96

Glossary 122

Conversion chart 125

Index 126

The oven temperatures in this book are for conventional ovens; if you have a fan-forced oven, decrease the oven temperature by 10-20 degrees.

pasta

carbonara gnocchi bake

1 tablespoon olive oil
1 medium brown onion (150g), chopped finely
3 cloves garlic, crushed
4 rindless bacon slices (260g), chopped coarsely
1½ cups (375ml) pouring cream
500g (1 pound) potato gnocchi
2 egg yolks
⅔ cup (50g) finely grated parmesan cheese
½ cup (35g) stale coarse breadcrumbs

1 Preheat oven to 200°C/400°F. Oil deep 1.5-litre (6-cup) ovenproof dish.
2 Heat oil in large frying pan; cook onion, garlic and bacon, stirring, until onion softens and bacon is crisp. Add cream; simmer, uncovered, about 5 minutes or until sauce thickens slightly. Season to taste. Cool.
3 Meanwhile, cook gnocchi in large saucepan of boiling water until tender; drain.
4 Combine gnocchi, sauce, egg yolks and half the cheese in large bowl; pour mixture into dish. Sprinkle with combined remaining cheese and breadcrumbs. Cover dish with foil; bake 25 minutes. Uncover; bake about 15 minutes or until browned.

prep + cook time 55 minutes **serves** 4
nutritional count per serving 59.2g total fat (33.2g saturated fat); 3511kJ (840 cal); 47.3g carbohydrate; 28.6g protein; 4.3g fibre

serving suggestion Serve with crusty bread and a leafy green salad.

seafood mornay lasagnes

6 lasagne sheets (170g)
60g (2 ounces) butter
⅓ cup (50g) plain (all-purpose) flour
2 cups (500ml) milk
½ cup (125ml) dry white wine
2 teaspoons finely grated lemon rind
¼ cup finely chopped fresh flat-leaf parsley
200g (6½ ounces) uncooked medium king prawns (shrimp)
200g (6½ ounces) firm white fish fillets
250g (8½ ounces) crab meat
½ cup (40g) finely grated parmesan cheese

1 Preheat oven to 220°C/425°F. Oil six 1¼-cup (310ml) ovenproof dishes.
2 Cook lasagne sheets, in batches, in large saucepan of boiling water until tender; drain. Cut each sheet into three squares.
3 Meanwhile, melt butter in large saucepan. Add flour; cook, stirring, about 2 minutes or until mixture bubbles and thickens. Gradually stir in milk and wine. Cook, stirring, until sauce boils and thickens; cool. Stir in rind and parsley; season to taste.
4 Shell and devein prawns; cut prawns and fish into 1cm (½-inch) pieces. Combine seafood in medium bowl.
5 Line base of each dish with one piece of lasagne. Top each with half the seafood, one-third of the sauce, then another piece of lasagne. Top each with remaining seafood, half the remaining sauce and another lasagne sheet. Top each with remaining sauce; sprinkle with cheese. Bake about 15 minutes or until seafood is cooked.

prep + cook time 45 minutes serves 6
nutritional count per serving 15.1g total fat (9.3g saturated fat); 1555kJ (372 cal); 30.6g carbohydrate; 25.1g protein; 1.4g fibre

notes Use fresh, instant or dried lasagne for this recipe. We used larger dishes here – each will serve three.

rocket pesto and spaghetti frittata

200g (6½ ounces) spaghetti
250g (8 ounces) rocket (arugula), chopped coarsely
2 tablespoons roasted pine nuts
¼ cup (20g) finely grated parmesan cheese
2 teaspoons finely grated lemon rind
2 cloves garlic, quartered
2 tablespoons olive oil
⅓ cup (50g) semi-dried tomatoes in oil, drained,
  chopped finely
6 eggs
1 cup (250ml) pouring cream

1 Preheat oven to 200°C/400°F. Oil deep 19cm (7½-inch)
square cake pan; line base and sides with baking paper,
extending paper 5cm (2 inches) over sides. Or, oil deep
ovenproof frying pan with base measuring 20cm (8 inches).
2 Cook pasta in large saucepan of boiling water until
tender; drain.
3 Meanwhile, blend or process rocket, nuts, cheese, rind,
garlic and oil until pesto is smooth.
4 Combine pasta, pesto and tomato in large bowl; season
to taste. Spread mixture into pan. Whisk eggs and cream
in large jug until combined; pour over pasta mixture. Bake
frittata, uncovered, about 35 minutes or until set. Stand
frittata in pan 5 minutes before cutting.

prep + cook time 55 minutes serves 6
nutritional count per serving 35.1g total fat
(15.4g saturated fat); 2057kJ (492 cal);
28.2g carbohydrate; 15.1g protein; 3.4g fibre

serving suggestion Serve with a garden salad.

spaghetti rosa bake

250g (8 ounces) spaghetti
1 tablespoon olive oil
1 medium brown onion (150g), chopped finely
2 cloves garlic, crushed
2⅔ cups (700g) bottled tomato pasta sauce
2 tablespoons finely chopped fresh basil
½ cup (125ml) pouring cream
1½ cups (150g) coarsely grated mozzarella cheese

1 Preheat oven to 200°C/400°F. Oil shallow 2-litre (8-cup) ovenproof dish.
2 Cook pasta in large saucepan of boiling water until tender; drain.
3 Meanwhile, heat oil in large saucepan; cook onion and garlic, stirring, until onion softens. Add sauce and basil; bring to the boil. Reduce heat; simmer, uncovered, about 10 minutes or until sauce is thickened slightly. Stir in cream; season.
4 Stir pasta and half the cheese into hot sauce in pan; spread mixture into dish. Sprinkle with remaining cheese. Bake about 20 minutes or until browned lightly.

prep + cook time 40 minutes **serves** 6
nutritional count per serving 19.9g total fat (10.1g saturated fat); 1668kJ (399 cal); 39.4g carbohydrate; 13.9g protein; 4.5g fibre

penne arrabbiata bake

300g (9½ ounces) penne pasta
1 tablespoon olive oil
1 medium brown onion (150g), chopped finely
3 cloves garlic, crushed
1 fresh long red chilli, chopped finely
6 drained anchovy fillets, chopped finely
2 tablespoons finely chopped fresh basil
2⅔ cups (700g) bottled tomato pasta sauce
½ cup (60g) seeded black olives, chopped coarsely
½ cup (55g) pizza cheese

1 Preheat oven to 180°C/350°F. Oil deep 2-litre (8-cup) ovenproof dish.
2 Cook pasta in large saucepan of boiling water until tender; drain.
3 Meanwhile, heat oil in large saucepan; cook onion, garlic, chilli, anchovy and basil, stirring, until onion softens. Add sauce; bring to the boil. Remove from heat; stir pasta and olives into hot sauce. Season to taste.
4 Spoon mixture into dish; sprinkle with cheese. Bake about 25 minutes or until browned lightly.

prep + cook time 45 minutes **serves** 4
nutritional count per serving 12g total fat
(3.1g saturated fat); 1977kJ (473 cal);
70.1g carbohydrate; 17.5g protein; 7.5g fibre

This recipe uses four lasagne sheets but only has three pasta layers. We used the fourth sheet to trim and fill any gaps in each pasta layer.

tomato, beef and pea lasagne

1 tablespoon olive oil
1 medium brown onion (150g), chopped finely
2 cloves garlic, crushed
500g (1 pound) minced (ground) beef
800g (1½ pounds) canned diced tomatoes
½ cup (125ml) beef stock
¼ cup (70g) tomato paste
2 tablespoons finely chopped fresh basil
1 cup (120g) frozen peas
60g (2 ounces) butter
⅓ cup (50g) plain (all-purpose) flour
3 cups (750ml) hot milk
1½ cups (150g) pizza cheese
4 fresh lasagne sheets

1 Heat oil in large frying pan; cook onion and garlic, stirring, until onion softens. Add beef; cook, stirring, until browned. Add undrained tomatoes, stock, paste and basil; bring to the boil. Reduce heat; simmer, covered, 30 minutes. Uncover; simmer, about 10 minutes or until sauce thickens slightly. Stir in peas; season to taste.
2 Meanwhile, melt butter in large saucepan. Add flour; cook, stirring, about 2 minutes or until mixture bubbles and thickens. Gradually stir in milk; cook, stirring, until sauce boils and thickens. Remove from heat; stir in half the cheese.
3 Preheat oven to 200°C/400°F. Oil deep 3.5-litre (14-cup) ovenproof dish.
4 Line base of dish with lasagne sheets, trimming to fit. Top with half the beef mixture, one-third of the cheese sauce, then more lasagne sheets, trimming to fit. Top with remaining beef mixture, half the remaining cheese sauce and remaining lasagne sheets, trimming to fit. Top with remaining cheese sauce; sprinkle with remaining cheese.
5 Cover lasagne with foil; bake 35 minutes. Uncover; bake about 20 minutes or until browned lightly. Stand lasagne 10 minutes before serving.

prep + cook time 1 hour 30 minutes serves 8
nutritional count per serving 19.2g total fat
(11.5g saturated fat); 1530kJ (366 cal);
22g carbohydrate; 25.3g protein; 3.6g fibre

asparagus, egg and bacon bake

250g (8 ounces) penne pasta
1 tablespoon olive oil
1 medium brown onion (150g), chopped finely
3 cloves garlic, crushed
3 rindless bacon slices (195g), sliced thinly
300g (9½ ounces) asparagus, trimmed, chopped coarsely
2 tablespoons plain (all-purpose) flour
½ cup (125ml) dry white wine
½ cup (125ml) chicken stock
1 cup (250ml) pouring cream
4 hard-boiled eggs, quartered
2 tablespoons finely chopped fresh chives
1 cup (80g) finely grated parmesan cheese
⅓ cup (25g) stale breadcrumbs

1 Preheat oven to 220°C/425°F. Oil deep 2.5-litre (10-cup) ovenproof dish.
2 Cook pasta in large saucepan of boiling water until tender; drain.
3 Meanwhile, heat oil in large saucepan; cook onion, garlic and bacon, stirring, until bacon is crisp. Add asparagus; cook, stirring, until tender. Add flour; cook, stirring, about 2 minutes or until mixture bubbles and thickens. Gradually stir in wine, stock and cream. Cook, stirring, until mixture boils and thickens.
4 Stir pasta, eggs, chives and half the cheese into asparagus mixture; season to taste. Spoon mixture into dish; sprinkle with combined remaining cheese and breadcrumbs. Bake about 20 minutes or until browned lightly.

prep + cook time 45 minutes serves 6
nutritional count per serving 32.6g total fat (17.4g saturated fat); 2345kJ (561 cal); 37.8g carbohydrate; 24.6g protein; 3.1g fibre

pumpkin, spinach and ricotta cannelloni

400g (12½ ounces) pumpkin, chopped coarsely
200g (6½ ounces) frozen spinach, thawed
200g (6½ ounces) ricotta cheese
12 cannelloni tubes (150g)
2⅔ cups (700g) bottled tomato pasta sauce
½ cup (60g) coarsely grated cheddar cheese
½ cup (40g) finely grated parmesan cheese

1 Preheat oven to 200°C/400°F. Oil shallow 1.5-litre (6-cup) ovenproof dish.
2 Boil, steam or microwave pumpkin until tender; drain. Mash pumpkin in medium bowl until smooth; cool.
3 Squeeze excess liquid from spinach; chop coarsely. Stir spinach and ricotta into pumpkin; season to taste. Fill cannelloni tubes with pumpkin mixture.
4 Spread half the sauce over base of dish; top with cannelloni, in single layer. Pour remaining sauce over cannelloni; sprinkle with combined cheddar and parmesan.
5 Cover dish with foil; bake 35 minutes. Uncover; bake about 20 minutes or until cannelloni are tender and cheese is browned lightly.

prep + cook time 1 hour 20 minutes serves 4
nutritional count per serving 17.8g total fat
(9.5g saturated fat); 1910kJ (457 cal);
46.3g carbohydrate; 23.7g protein; 9g fibre

serving suggestion Serve with a leafy green salad.
note We used butternut pumpkin for this recipe.

spinach and ricotta pasta slice

300g (9½ ounces) angel hair pasta
410g (13 ounces) canned tomato puree
150g (4½ ounces) baby spinach leaves
300g (9½ ounces) ricotta cheese
4 eggs
½ cup (125ml) pouring cream
½ cup (55g) pizza cheese

1 Preheat oven to 200°C/400°F. Oil shallow 2-litre (8-cup) ovenproof dish.
2 Cook pasta in large saucepan of boiling water until tender; drain, cool.
3 Spread one-third of the tomato puree over base of dish; top with half the spinach, half the pasta and half the ricotta. Pour half the remaining tomato puree over ricotta; top with remaining spinach and remaining pasta. Pour remaining tomato puree over pasta; sprinkle with remaining ricotta.
4 Whisk eggs and cream in large jug until combined; season. Pour egg mixture over pasta; sprinkle with pizza cheese. Bake, uncovered, about 40 minutes or until browned lightly and set.

prep + cook time 1 hour **serves** 6
nutritional count per serving 20.9g total fat (12g saturated fat); 1802kJ (431 cal); 39.1g carbohydrate; 19.9g protein; 3.6g fibre

broccoli and cheese penne with garlic and lemon crumbs

200g (6½ ounces) penne pasta
500g (1 pound) broccoli, cut into small florets
3 eggs
1 cup (250ml) pouring cream
⅓ cup (80ml) milk
⅔ cup (80g) coarsely grated cheddar cheese
½ cup (35g) stale breadcrumbs
1 cup (80g) finely grated parmesan cheese
2 cloves garlic, crushed
1 tablespoon finely grated lemon rind
2 tablespoons finely chopped fresh flat-leaf parsley

1 Preheat oven to 220°C/425°F. Oil deep 2-litre (8-cup) ovenproof dish.
2 Cook pasta in large saucepan of boiling water until tender. Add broccoli for last 5 minutes of pasta cooking time; drain. Rinse pasta and broccoli under cold water; drain, cool.
3 Combine pasta, broccoli, eggs, cream, milk and cheddar in large bowl; season. Spoon mixture into dish; sprinkle with combined breadcrumbs, parmesan, garlic, rind and parsley. Bake, uncovered, about 40 minutes or until browned lightly and set. Stand 10 minutes before serving.

prep + cook time 1 hour **serves** 6
nutritional count per serving 30.5g total fat
(18.8g saturated fat); 2048kJ (490 cal);
29.3g carbohydrate; 21.6g protein; 5.1g fibre

pastitsio

1 tablespoon olive oil
1 medium brown onion (150g), chopped finely
2 cloves garlic, crushed
500g (1 pound) minced (ground) beef
1 teaspoon ground cinnamon
½ teaspoon ground nutmeg
800g (1½ pounds) canned diced tomatoes
½ cup (125ml) dry white wine
½ cup (125ml) beef stock
¼ cup (70g) tomato paste
2 tablespoons finely chopped fresh flat-leaf parsley
200g (6½ ounces) macaroni pasta
1 egg
1 cup (80g) finely grated parmesan cheese
¼ cup (15g) stale breadcrumbs

CHEESE TOPPING
60g (2 ounces) butter
⅓ cup (50g) plain (all-purpose) flour
2 cups (500ml) hot milk
1 cup (80g) finely grated parmesan cheese
1 egg yolk

1 Heat oil in large frying pan; cook onion and garlic, stirring, until onion softens. Add beef and spices; cook, stirring, until browned and fragrant. Add undrained tomatoes, wine, stock and paste; bring to the boil. Reduce heat; simmer, covered, 30 minutes. Uncover; simmer, about 5 minutes or until sauce thickens slightly. Stir in parsley; season to taste.
2 Meanwhile, make cheese topping.
3 Preheat oven to 200°C/400°F. Oil shallow 2-litre (8-cup) ovenproof dish.
4 Cook pasta in large saucepan of boiling water until tender; drain. Combine pasta and egg in large bowl. Spoon pasta mixture into dish; top with beef mixture. Spread cheese topping over beef mixture; sprinkle with combined cheese and breadcrumbs. Bake, uncovered, about 25 minutes or until browned lightly. Stand 5 minutes before serving.

CHEESE TOPPING Melt butter in medium saucepan. Add flour; cook, stirring, about 2 minutes or until mixture bubbles and thickens. Gradually stir in milk; cook, stirring, until sauce boils and thickens. Remove from heat; stir in cheese and egg yolk.

prep + cook time 1 hour 30 minutes serves 6
nutritional count per serving 32.2g total fat
(17.3g saturated fat); 2638kJ (631 cal);
41.7g carbohydrate; 38.4g protein; 4.2g fibre

classic macaroni cheese

375g (12 ounces) macaroni pasta
60g (2 ounces) butter
¼ cup (35g) plain (all-purpose) flour
3 cups (750ml) hot milk
1½ cups (180g) coarsely grated cheddar cheese
1 cup (70g) stale coarse white breadcrumbs

1   Preheat oven to 180°C/350°F. Oil 1.5-litre (6-cup) ovenproof dish.
2   Cook pasta in large saucepan of boiling water until tender; drain.

3   Meanwhile, melt butter in large saucepan. Add flour; cook, stirring, about 2 minutes or until mixture bubbles and thickens. Gradually stir in milk. Cook, stirring, until sauce boils and thickens. Stir in 1 cup of the cheese.
4   Stir pasta into hot sauce mixture; spoon into dish. Sprinkle with combined breadcrumbs and remaining cheese. Bake, uncovered, about 25 minutes or until browned lightly.

prep + cook time 1 hour **serves** 4
nutritional count per serving 36.5g total fat (22.9g saturated fat); 3432kJ (821 cal); 89.7g carbohydrate; 31.5g protein; 4.1g fibre

note We used ciabatta bread to make the breadcrumbs.

tuna mornay with pasta YUM!

375g (12 ounces) elbow pasta
60g (2 ounces) butter
1 medium brown onion (150g), chopped finely
1 clove garlic, crushed
2 stalks celery (300g), trimmed, chopped finely
¼ cup (35g) plain (all-purpose) flour
1½ cups (375ml) hot milk
1 cup (250ml) pouring cream
425g (13½ ounces) canned tuna in springwater,
    drained, flaked
2 tablespoons finely chopped fresh flat-leaf parsley
2 teaspoons finely grated lemon rind
1 cup (70g) stale coarse breadcrumbs
1 cup (120g) coarsely grated cheddar cheese

1 Preheat oven to 180°C/350°F. Oil deep 2.5-litre (10-cup) ovenproof dish.
2 Cook pasta in large saucepan of boiling water until tender; drain.
3 Melt butter in large saucepan; cook onion, garlic and celery, stirring, until onion softens. Add flour; cook, stirring, about 2 minutes or until mixture bubbles and thickens. Gradually stir in milk and cream. Cook, stirring, until sauce boils and thickens.
4 Stir pasta, tuna, parsley and rind into sauce mixture; season. Spoon mixture into dish; sprinkle with combined breadcrumbs and cheese. Bake, uncovered, about 35 minutes or until browned lightly.

prep + cook time 1 hour **serves** 6
nutritional count per serving 38g total fat
(24g saturated fat); 2997kJ (717 cal);
61.1g carbohydrate; 31g protein; 3.8g fibre

creamy bolognese pasta bake

1 tablespoon olive oil
1 medium brown onion (150g), chopped finely
3 cloves garlic, crushed
2 stalks celery (300g), trimmed, chopped finely
1 large carrot (180g), chopped finely
500g (1 pound) minced (ground) beef
½ cup (125ml) dry red wine
½ cup (125ml) beef stock
410g (13 ounces) canned diced tomatoes
⅓ cup (95g) tomato paste
1 cup (250ml) milk
½ cup (60g) frozen peas
¼ cup finely chopped fresh flat-leaf parsley
300g (9½ ounces) rigatoni pasta
1½ cups (180g) coarsely grated cheddar cheese

1 Heat oil in large saucepan; cook onion, garlic, celery and carrot, stirring, until vegetables soften. Add beef; cook, stirring, until browned. Add wine; bring to the boil. Boil, uncovered, until liquid is almost evaporated. Add stock, undrained tomatoes, paste and milk; bring to the boil. Reduce heat; simmer, uncovered, about 30 minutes or until sauce thickens slightly. Stir in peas and parsley; season to taste.
2 Preheat oven to 220°C/425°F. Oil deep 3-litre (12-cup) ovenproof dish.
3 Cook pasta in large saucepan of boiling water until tender; drain.
4 Stir pasta into bolognese mixture with half the cheese. Spoon mixture into dish; sprinkle with remaining cheese. Bake, uncovered, about 15 minutes or until browned lightly. Stand 5 minutes before serving.

prep + cook time 1 hour 10 minutes serves 6
nutritional count per serving 22g total fat
(11.2g saturated fat); 2245kJ (537 cal);
44.2g carbohydrate; 34g protein; 5.8g fibre

vegetables

spinach and kumara gnocchi

1kg (2 pounds) kumara (orange sweet potato),
    chopped coarsely
2 medium potatoes (400g), chopped coarsely
½ cup finely chopped spinach leaves
1 cup (150g) plain (all-purpose) flour, approximately
½ cup (40g) finely grated parmesan cheese

TOMATO BASIL SAUCE
1 tablespoon olive oil
1 small brown onion (80g), chopped finely
2 cloves garlic, crushed
4 medium tomatoes (600g), chopped finely
¼ cup finely chopped fresh basil

1   Preheat oven to 200°C/400°F. Oil six shallow 1½-cup (375ml) ovenproof dishes.
2   Roast kumara and potato, in single layer, on oiled oven tray, about 40 minutes or until tender; cool.
3   Meanwhile, make tomato basil sauce.
4   Push kumara and potato through potato ricer or sieve into large bowl. Stir in spinach and enough of the sifted flour to make a soft, sticky dough.
5   To make gnocchi flatten dough on floured surface to 1cm (½-inch) thickness. Cut 5cm (2-inch) rounds from dough; transfer gnocchi to tea-towel-lined tray. Reshape and cut rounds from any remaining dough until all dough is used.
6   Cook gnocchi, in batches, in large saucepan of boiling water until gnocchi float to the surface and are cooked through. Remove gnocchi using slotted spoon; transfer to dishes. Top with sauce, sprinkle with cheese. Bake, uncovered, about 15 minutes or until browned lightly.

TOMATO BASIL SAUCE   Heat oil in medium saucepan; cook onion and garlic, stirring, until onion softens. Add tomato; cook, stirring, about 5 minutes or until tomato softens. Simmer, uncovered, 10 minutes or until sauce thickens slightly. Stir in basil; season to taste.

prep + cook time 1 hour 30 minutes serves 6
nutritional count per serving 5.8g total fat
(1.9g saturated fat); 1233kJ (295 cal);
46.6g carbohydrate; 10.4g protein; 5.9g fibre

note You will need to buy one bunch of spinach (300g/9½ ounces) to make this recipe.

curried lentil pies

2 tablespoons ghee
1 medium brown onion (150g), chopped finely
2 cloves garlic, crushed
4cm (1½-inch) piece fresh ginger (20g), grated
1 fresh long red chilli, chopped finely
1 stalk celery (150g), trimmed, chopped coarsely
1 large carrot (180g), chopped coarsely
2 teaspoons each black mustard seeds, ground cumin
   and ground coriander
1 teaspoon ground turmeric
1½ cups (300g) brown lentils
410g (13 ounces) canned crushed tomatoes
2 cups (500ml) vegetable stock
⅔ cup (160ml) coconut milk
½ cup (60g) frozen peas
½ cup coarsely chopped fresh coriander (cilantro)
600g (1¼ pounds) pumpkin, chopped coarsely
2 medium potatoes (400g), chopped coarsely
60g (2 ounces) butter

1 Heat ghee in large saucepan; cook onion, garlic, ginger, chilli, celery and carrot, stirring, until vegetables soften. Add spices; cook, stirring, until fragrant. Add lentils, undrained tomatoes and stock; simmer, covered, stirring occasionally, about 1 hour or until lentils are tender. Stir in coconut milk, peas and coriander; season to taste.
2 Meanwhile, boil, steam or microwave pumpkin and potato until tender; drain. Mash pumpkin and potato with butter in medium bowl until smooth.
3 Preheat oven to 220°C/425°F. Oil four deep 1¼-cup (310ml) ovenproof dishes.
4 Divide lentil mixture among dishes; top with pumpkin mixture. Bake, uncovered, about 20 minutes or until browned lightly. Sprinkle with black sesame seeds if you like.

prep + cook time 1 hour serves 4
nutritional count per serving 31.9g total fat
(21.7g saturated fat); 2796kJ (669 cal);
60.3g carbohydrate; 28.3g protein; 18.9g fibre

eggplant parmigiana

2 medium eggplants (600g)
2 teaspoons coarse cooking (kosher) salt
1 tablespoon olive oil
1 medium brown onion (150g), chopped finely
2 cloves garlic, crushed
2 tablespoons finely chopped fresh basil
2⅔ cups (700g) bottled tomato pasta sauce
1½ cups (150g) coarsely grated mozzarella cheese
½ cup (40g) finely grated parmesan cheese
½ cup (35g) stale coarse breadcrumbs

1 Peel and discard strips of skin from eggplant; cut eggplant into 5mm (¼-inch) slices. Place eggplant in colander; sprinkle with salt. Stand in sink 30 minutes. Rinse eggplant under cold water; drain. Squeeze excess water from eggplant.
2 Meanwhile, heat oil in medium saucepan; cook onion, garlic and basil, stirring, until onion softens. Add sauce; bring to the boil. Reduce heat; simmer, uncovered, about 15 minutes or until sauce thickens slightly. Season to taste.
3 Preheat oven to 220°C/425°F. Oil six 1¼-cup (310ml) ovenproof dishes.
4 Spoon half the sauce into dishes; top with half the eggplant and half the mozzarella. Top with remaining eggplant, remaining sauce, then remaining mozzarella. Sprinkle with combined parmesan and breadcrumbs.
5 Cover dishes with foil; place on oven tray. Bake about 40 minutes or until eggplant is tender. Uncover; bake about 15 minutes or until browned lightly.

prep + cook time 1 hour 15 minutes serves 6
nutritional count per serving 13.2g total fat
(5.5g saturated fat); 1041kJ (249 cal);
16.9g carbohydrate; 13.4g protein; 5.6g fibre

note We've used larger dishes here – each dish will serve three.

root vegetable gratin

2 medium potatoes (400g)
2 medium carrots (240g)
2 medium parsnips (500g)
1 small brown onion (80g)
⅔ cup (160ml) pouring cream
⅔ cup (160ml) milk
2 tablespoons finely chopped fresh flat-leaf parsley
1 tablespoon horseradish cream
⅓ cup (25g) stale breadcrumbs

1 Preheat oven to 200°C/400°F. Oil deep 1.5 litre (6-cup) ovenproof dish.
2 Using mandolin or V-slicer, cut potato, carrot, parsnip and onion into paper-thin slices. Place potato over base of dish; top with half the onion. Top with carrot, then remaining onion and parsnip.
3 Combine cream, milk, parsley and horseradish cream in large jug; season. Pour cream mixture over vegetables; sprinkle with breadcrumbs.
4 Cover dish with foil; bake about 1¼ hours or until vegetables are tender. Uncover; bake about 30 minutes or until browned lightly. Stand 5 minutes before serving.

prep + cook time 2 hours **serves** 4
nutritional count per serving 20g total fat (12.8g saturated fat); 1496kJ (358 cal); 33.8g carbohydrate; 7.8g protein; 6.3g fibre

cheese and vegetable polenta bake

45g (1½ ounces) butter
1 medium brown onion (150g), chopped finely
1 clove garlic, crushed
1 medium eggplant (300g), chopped finely
1 medium red capsicum (bell pepper) (200g),
  chopped finely
1 medium green capsicum (bell pepper) (200g),
  chopped finely
100g (3 ounces) button mushrooms, chopped finely
410g (13 ounces) canned crushed tomatoes
2 tablespoons finely chopped fresh basil
1 litre (4 cups) water
1⅓ cups (225g) polenta
½ cup (40g) finely grated parmesan cheese
½ cup (60g) coarsely grated cheddar cheese

1 Preheat oven to 220°C/425°F. Oil deep 1.75-litre (7-cup)
ovenproof dish.
2 Melt butter in large frying pan; cook onion and garlic,
stirring, until onion softens. Add eggplant, capsicum,
mushrooms and undrained tomatoes; bring to the boil.
Reduce heat; simmer, uncovered, about 15 minutes or
until vegetables are tender and sauce thickens slightly.
Remove from heat; stir in basil. Season to taste.
3 Meanwhile, bring the water to the boil in medium
saucepan; gradually stir in polenta. Cook, stirring,
about 5 minutes or until polenta thickens. Stir in
cheeses; season to taste.
4 Spread half the polenta mixture over base of dish;
top with vegetable mixture. Spread remaining polenta
mixture over vegetables. Bake about 20 minutes or until
browned lightly. Stand 5 minutes before serving.

prep + cook time 55 minutes serves 4
nutritional count per serving 19.3g total fat
(11.5g saturated fat); 1877kJ (449 cal);
49g carbohydrate; 16.6g protein; 6.5g fibre

vegie casserole with chive dumplings

1 tablespoon olive oil
1 large leek (500g), sliced thinly
2 cloves garlic, crushed
3 rindless bacon slices (195g), chopped coarsely
2 stalks celery (300g), trimmed, chopped coarsely
1 large carrot (180g), chopped coarsely
2 medium red capsicums (bell peppers) (400g),
  chopped coarsely
2 medium zucchini (240g), chopped coarsely
½ cup (125ml) dry red wine
410g (13 ounces) canned crushed tomatoes
1 cup (250ml) water
400g (12½ ounces) swiss brown mushrooms, halved
½ cup (60g) frozen peas

CHIVE DUMPLINGS
1½ cups (225g) self-raising flour
60g (2 ounces) butter, chopped finely
¾ cup (60g) finely grated parmesan cheese
2 tablespoons finely chopped fresh chives
½ cup (125ml) milk, approximately

1 Preheat oven to 180°C/350°F.
2 Heat oil in large flameproof casserole dish; cook leek, garlic and bacon, stirring, until leek softens and bacon is crisp. Add celery, carrot, capsicum, zucchini, wine, undrained tomatoes and the water; bring to the boil. Cover; bake about 20 minutes or until vegetables are tender.
3 Meanwhile, make chive dumplings.
4 Remove dish from oven; stir in mushrooms and peas. Season. Drop level tablespoons of dumpling mixture on top of stew.
5 Bake, uncovered, about 20 minutes or until dumplings are puffed and browned lightly.

CHIVE DUMPLINGS Sift flour into medium bowl; rub in butter. Stir in cheese and chives, then enough milk to make a soft sticky dough.

prep + cook time 45 minutes serves 6
nutritional count per serving 19.6g total fat
(9.6g saturated fat); 1910kJ (457 cal);
39.8g carbohydrate; 22g protein; 9.9g fibre

pumpkin, pea and fetta risotto

500g (1 pound) pumpkin, chopped coarsely
1 tablespoon olive oil
2 cups (500ml) chicken stock
2 cups (500ml) water
1 medium brown onion (150g), chopped finely
2 cloves garlic, crushed
1½ cups (300g) arborio rice
250g (8 ounces) grape tomatoes
1 cup (120g) frozen peas
⅓ cup (25g) finely grated parmesan cheese
100g (3 ounces) soft fetta cheese, crumbled
1 tablespoon coarsely chopped fresh marjoram

1 Preheat oven to 220°C/425°F.
2 Combine pumpkin and half the oil in medium shallow flameproof casserole dish. Roast, uncovered, about 20 minutes or until tender; remove from dish.
3 Reduce oven to 180°C/350°F.
4 Bring stock and the water to the boil in medium saucepan. Reduce heat; simmer, covered.
5 Meanwhile, heat remaining oil in same dish; cook onion and garlic, stirring, until onion softens. Add rice; stir to coat in onion mixture. Stir in simmering stock mixture; cover dish with foil.
6 Bake 25 minutes, stirring halfway through cooking time. Remove risotto from oven; stir in tomatoes and peas. Bake, uncovered, about 10 minutes or until rice is tender. Stir in pumpkin and parmesan; season to taste. Sprinkle with fetta and marjoram.

prep + cook time 1 hour serves 4
nutritional count per serving 13.9g total fat (6.4g saturated fat); 2123kJ (508 cal); 73.7g carbohydrate; 18.4g protein; 6.1g fibre

cauliflower and broccoli gratin

½ small cauliflower (500g), cut into large florets
400g (12½ ounces) broccoli, cut into large florets
60g (2 ounces) butter
¼ cup (35g) plain (all-purpose) flour
3 cups (750ml) hot milk
1 cup (120g) coarsely grated cheddar cheese
½ cup (35g) stale breadcrumbs
½ cup (40g) finely grated parmesan cheese

1   Preheat oven to 220°C/425°F. Oil shallow 1.75-litre (7-cup) ovenproof dish.
2   Boil, steam or microwave cauliflower and broccoli, separately, until tender; drain.
3   Meanwhile, melt butter in large saucepan. Add flour; cook, stirring, about 2 minutes or until mixture bubbles and thickens. Gradually stir in milk; cook, stirring, until sauce boils and thickens. Stir in cheddar; season to taste.
4   Place cauliflower and broccoli in dish, pour cheese sauce over; sprinkle with combined breadcrumbs and parmesan. Bake, uncovered, about 20 minutes or until browned lightly.

prep + cook time 45 minutes **serves** 6 (as a side dish)
nutritional count per serving 22.7g total fat (14.3g saturated fat); 1484kJ (355 cal); 16.4g carbohydrate; 19.1g protein; 5.4g fibre

notes To prevent excess water leaching into the gratin, steaming is the best method to use for cooking the vegetables. You can use broccolini instead of broccoli, if you prefer.
We've used two ovenproof pans here – each pan will serve three.

fennel and leek gratin

4 baby fennel bulbs (520g)
1 medium leek (350g), sliced thinly
1½ cups (375ml) pouring cream
½ cup (125ml) milk
45g (1½ ounces) butter
2 tablespoons plain (all-purpose) flour
⅓ cup (40g) coarsely grated cheddar cheese
⅓ cup (25g) finely grated parmesan cheese
⅔ cup (50g) stale breadcrumbs

1 Trim and quarter fennel; reserve 1 tablespoon finely chopped fennel fronds.
2 Combine fennel, leek, cream and milk in large saucepan; simmer, covered, about 15 minutes or until fennel is tender. Transfer fennel and leek to six shallow 1-cup (250ml) ovenproof dishes; reserve cream mixture.
3 Preheat oven to 220°C/425°F.
4 Melt butter in same pan. Add flour; cook, stirring, about 2 minutes or until mixture bubbles and thickens. Gradually stir in hot cream mixture. Cook, stirring, until sauce boils and thickens; season to taste.
5 Pour sauce over fennel; sprinkle with combined cheeses, breadcrumbs and reserved fennel fronds. Bake, uncovered, about 15 minutes or until browned lightly.

prep + cook time 45 minutes **serves** 6 (as a side dish)
nutritional count per serving 38.2g total fat (24.8g saturated fat); 1839kJ (440 cal); 15.2g carbohydrate; 8.5g protein; 3.7g fibre

serving suggestion Serve with roast lamb, beef or veal, or your favourite steak.

potatoes

potato gratin with caramelised onion

1 tablespoon olive oil
2 large brown onions (400g), sliced thinly
1 tablespoon light brown sugar
3 teaspoons balsamic vinegar
2 tablespoons coarsely chopped fresh flat-leaf parsley
1kg (2 pounds) potatoes
1 tablespoon plain (all-purpose) flour
1¾ cups (430ml) pouring cream
¼ cup (60ml) milk
20g (¾ ounce) butter, chopped finely
¾ cup (90g) coarsely grated gruyère cheese
¾ cup (50g) stale breadcrumbs

1 Heat oil in medium frying pan over low heat; cook onion, stirring occasionally, about 20 minutes or until onion softens. Add sugar and vinegar; cook, stirring occasionally, about 10 minutes or until onion is caramelised. Remove from heat; stir in parsley.
2 Preheat oven to 180°C/350°F. Oil 1.5-litre (6-cup) ovenproof dish.
3 Using mandolin or V-slicer, cut potatoes into paper thin slices; pat dry with absorbent paper. Layer half the potato in dish; top with caramelised onion, then remaining potato.
4 Blend flour with a little of the cream in medium jug; stir in remaining cream and milk. Pour cream mixture over potato mixture; dot with butter. Cover with foil; bake 1¼ hours. Uncover; sprinkle with combined cheese and breadcrumbs. Bake, uncovered, about 15 minutes or until potato is tender. Stand 5 minutes before serving.

prep + cook time 1 hour 45 minutes serves 6
nutritional count per serving 42.1g total fat (25.8g saturated fat); 2337kJ (559 cal); 32.9g carbohydrate; 11.5g protein; 3.5g fibre

note We used sebago potatoes in this recipe.

potatoes with lemon and tomato

1.2kg (2½ pounds) medium potatoes, cut into
 thick wedges
2 medium lemons (280g), sliced thickly
1 tablespoon fresh thyme leaves
½ cup (125ml) dry white wine
2 tablespoons olive oil
480g (15½ ounces) cherry truss tomatoes, cut into
 5cm (2-inch) lengths
½ cup (80g) seeded kalamata olives
2 tablespoons coarsely chopped fresh flat-leaf parsley

1 Preheat oven to 200°C/400°F. Oil 2.5-litre (10-cup)
ovenproof dish.
2 Combine potato, lemon and thyme in dish; pour
over combined wine and oil. Season. Cover dish with
foil; bake 40 minutes. Uncover; bake 30 minutes. Remove
from oven; top with tomatoes. Bake, uncovered, further
12 minutes or until potato is tender.
3 Serve sprinkled with olives and parsley.

prep + cook time 1 hour 35 minutes serves 6
nutritional count per serving 6.6g total fat
(0.9g saturated fat); 903kJ (216 cal);
26.8g carbohydrate; 4.7g protein; 5.2g fibre

serving suggestion Serve with grilled or barbecued
chicken or fish.

potato, bacon and blue cheese bake

1.2kg (2½ pounds) medium potatoes, sliced thickly
2 medium red onions (340g), cut into thick wedges
315g (10 ounces) rindless bacon slices, chopped coarsely
12 sprigs fresh thyme
¾ cup (180ml) pouring cream
¾ cup (180ml) salt-reduced chicken stock
125g (4 ounces) blue cheese, crumbled

1 Preheat oven to 200°C/400°F. Oil 2.5-litre (10-cup) ovenproof dish.
2 Combine potato, onion and bacon in dish; top with half the thyme. Combine cream and stock in medium jug; season, pour over potato.
3 Bake, uncovered, about 1½ hours or until potato is tender. Serve topped with cheese and remaining thyme.

prep + cook time 1 hour 45 minutes **serves** 6
nutritional count per serving 22.9g total fat
(13.5g saturated fat); 1659kJ (397 cal);
25.6g carbohydrate; 20.5g protein; 3.3g fibre

potato gnocchi with three-cheese sauce

500g (1 pound) potatoes, unpeeled
1 egg, beaten lightly
15g (½ ounce) butter, melted
2 tablespoons finely grated parmesan cheese
1 cup (150g) plain (all-purpose) flour, approximately
¼ cup (25g) stale coarse breadcrumbs

THREE-CHEESE SAUCE
1 cup (250ml) pouring cream
½ cup (50g) coarsely grated mozzarella cheese
45g (1½ ounces) gorgonzola cheese, crumbled
½ cup (40g) finely grated parmesan cheese
1 teaspoon dijon mustard
¼ teaspoon ground nutmeg
1 egg yolk
1 tablespoon finely chopped fresh curly parsley

1 Boil or steam whole potatoes until tender; drain. When cool enough to handle, peel away skins. Mash potatoes, using ricer, food mill (mouli) or strainer, into medium bowl; stir in egg, butter, cheese and enough flour to make a firm dough.
2 Divide dough into four portions; roll each portion on floured surface into 2cm (¾in) thick sausage shape. Cut each sausage into 2cm (¾in) pieces; roll pieces into balls.
3 Roll each ball along the tines of a fork, pressing lightly on top of ball with index finger to form classic gnocchi shape – grooved on one side and dimpled on the other. Place gnocchi, in single layer, on lightly floured tray; cover, refrigerate 1 hour.
4 Meanwhile, make three-cheese sauce.
5 Preheat oven to 220°C/425°F. Oil four 1-cup (250ml) ovenproof dishes.
6 Cook gnocchi, in batches, in large saucepan of boiling water until gnocchi float to the surface and are cooked through. Remove from pan with slotted spoon; divide among dishes. Pour sauce over gnocchi; sprinkle with breadcrumbs. Bake, uncovered, about 15 minutes.

THREE-CHEESE SAUCE Combine cream and cheeses in small saucepan; stir over medium heat until smooth. Remove from heat; stir in mustard, nutmeg, egg yolk and parsley. Season to taste.

prep + cook time 1 hour (+ refrigeration) serves 4
nutritional count per serving 44.3g total fat
(27.8g saturated fat); 2537kJ (607 cal);
33.2g carbohydrate; 19.3g protein; 1.8g fibre

serving suggestion Serve with a green salad.
note We used russet burbank potatoes in this recipe.

mashed potato and bacon bake

2kg (4 pounds) potatoes, chopped coarsely
410g (13 ounces) rindless bacon slices, chopped finely
1 cup (240g) sour cream
90g (3 ounces) butter, chopped coarsely
¾ cup (180ml) hot milk
4 green onions (scallions), sliced thinly
2 cups (240g) coarsely grated cheddar cheese

1 Preheat oven to 180°C/350°F. Oil 2.5-litre (10-cup) ovenproof dish.
2 Boil steam or microwave potato until tender; drain.
3 Meanwhile, cook bacon in large frying pan, stirring, until crisp; drain on absorbent paper.
4 Mash potato in large bowl with sour cream, butter and milk until smooth. Stir in half the bacon, half the onion and half the cheese. Season to taste. Spread mixture into dish; sprinkle with remaining bacon, onion and cheese. Bake, uncovered, about 40 minutes or until browned lightly.

prep + cook time 1 hour 20 minutes serves 8
nutritional count per serving 36.9g total fat (22.6g saturated fat); 2303kJ (551 cal); 28.9g carbohydrate; 24.5g protein; 3.3g fibre

potato frittata

2 tablespoons olive oil
625g (1¼ pounds) potatoes, chopped coarsely
45g (1½ ounces) baby spinach leaves
2 tablespoons coarsely chopped fresh flat-leaf parsley
125g (4 ounces) goat's fetta cheese, crumbled
⅓ cup (25g) coarsely grated parmesan cheese
6 eggs
½ cup (125ml) pouring cream

1 Preheat oven to 200°C/400°F. Oil deep 20cm (8-inch) square cake pan; line base and sides with baking paper; extending paper 5cm (2 inches) over sides. Or, oil deep ovenproof frying pan with base measuring 20cm (8 inches).

2 Heat oil in large frying pan; cook potato, stirring, until browned lightly and almost tender. Drain on absorbent paper.
3 Layer half the spinach, parsley, potato and cheeses in pan; repeat layers. Combine eggs and cream in medium jug; season. Pour egg mixture into pan. Bake about 30 minutes or until set. Stand 5 minutes before serving.

prep + cook time 50 minutes **serves** 4
nutritional count per serving 39.8g total fat (18.6g saturated fat); 2169kJ (519 cal); 17.8g carbohydrate; 21.7g protein; 2.4g fibre

note We used desiree potatoes in this recipe.

twice-baked potatoes

8 medium potatoes (1.6kg), unpeeled
200g (6½ ounces) rindless bacon slices, chopped finely
125g (4 ounces) canned creamed corn
¼ cup (60g) sour cream
2 green onions (scallions), sliced thinly
1 cup (120g) coarsely grated cheddar cheese

1 Preheat oven to 180°C/350°F.
2 Pierce skin of each potato with a skewer or fork; wrap each potato in foil, place in baking-paper-lined large shallow baking dish. Bake, uncovered, about 1 hour and 20 minutes or until tender.
3 Meanwhile, cook bacon in medium frying pan until crisp. Drain on absorbent paper.
4 Cut a shallow slice from each potato; scoop flesh from each top into medium bowl, discard skin. Scoop about two-thirds of the flesh from each potato into same bowl; place potato shells in same baking dish.
5 Mash potato until smooth; stir in creamed corn, sour cream, bacon, half the onion and half the cheese. Divide mixture into potato shells; sprinkle with remaining onion and cheese. Bake, uncovered, about 20 minutes or until heated through.

prep + cook time 1 hour 55 minutes serves 4
nutritional count per serving 21g total fat
(12g saturated fat); 2115kJ (506 cal);
48.3g carbohydrate; 26.6g protein; 6.3g fibre

ham, potato, leek and artichoke bake

45g (1½ ounces) butter
2 tablespoons plain (all-purpose) flour
2 cups (500ml) hot chicken stock
1kg (2 pounds) potatoes, sliced thickly
2 medium leeks (700g), sliced thickly
200g (6½ ounces) leg ham, chopped coarsely
280g (9 ounces) bottled artichoke hearts in brine,
 drained, halved
1 cup (80g) coarsely grated parmesan cheese

1 Preheat oven to 200°C/400°F. Oil 2-litre (8-cup)
ovenproof dish.
2 Melt butter in medium saucepan. Add flour; cook,
stirring, about 2 minutes or until mixture bubbles and
thickens. Gradually stir in stock; cook sauce, stirring,
until mixture boils and thickens. Season to taste.
3 Layer half the potato in dish; top with leek, ham,
artichokes and the remaining potato. Pour sauce over
potato. Cover dish with foil; bake 1 hour 20 minutes.
Uncover; sprinkle with cheese. Bake about 30 minutes or
until potato is tender. Stand 10 minutes before serving.

prep + cook time 2 hours serves 8
nutritional count per serving 9.6g total fat
(5.6g saturated fat); 970kJ (232 cal);
19.6g carbohydrate; 14.2g protein; 5.1g fibre

seafood

salmon and zucchini lasagne

45g (1½ ounces) butter
¼ cup (35g) plain (all-purpose) flour
2 cups (500ml) hot milk
1 cup (240g) ricotta cheese
3 green onions (scallions), chopped finely
2 tablespoons finely chopped fresh mint
2 large zucchini (300g), sliced thinly lengthways
3 fresh lasagne sheets (150g)
400g (12½ ounces) skinless salmon fillet, sliced thinly
½ cup (50g) coarsely grated mozzarella cheese

1 Preheat oven to 220°C/425°F.
2 Melt butter in medium saucepan. Add flour; cook, stirring, about 2 minutes or until mixture bubbles and thickens. Gradually stir in milk; cook, stirring, until sauce boils and thickens. Season to taste. Spoon 1 cup white sauce into medium bowl; stir in ricotta, onion and mint.
3 Cook zucchini in large saucepan of boiling, salted water for 2 minutes. Drain zucchini in a single layer on absorbent paper. Cook pasta, in batches, in same pan of boiling water for about 30 seconds or until tender; drain.
4 Spread ⅓ cup white sauce over base of 1-litre (4-cup) ovenproof dish. Top with a lasagne sheet, half the zucchini, then half the fish and half the ricotta mixture. Repeat layering, seasoning lightly between layers, with remaining lasagne, zucchini, fish and ricotta mixture, finishing with a lasagne sheet. Top with remaining white sauce; sprinkle with mozzarella. Bake, uncovered, about 20 minutes or until browned lightly.

prep + cook time 50 minutes serves 4
nutritional count per serving 31.5g total fat
(17.1g saturated fat); 2541kJ (608 cal);
40.4g carbohydrate; 39.6g protein; 3.1g fibre

notes To ensure the fish doesn't overcook during the baking time, you need to pre-cook the zucchini and pasta. As cooked, drained lasagne sheets tend to stick together, it's better to cook each sheet just before using it.

tuna and asparagus crumble

45g (1½ ounces) butter
2 medium leeks (700g), chopped finely
340g (11 ounces) asparagus, chopped coarsely
1 cup (250ml) pouring cream
425g (13½ ounces) canned tuna in springwater,
  drained, flaked

CRUMBLE OAT TOPPING
⅔ cup (60g) rolled oats
⅓ cup (40g) coarsely grated cheddar cheese
2 tablespoons plain (all-purpose) flour
30g (1 ounce) butter, chopped finely

1 Make crumble oat topping.
2 Preheat oven to 240°C/475°F.
3 Melt butter in large frying pan; cook leek, stirring,
2 minutes. Add asparagus; cook, covered, about
5 minutes or until asparagus is tender. Add cream
and tuna; bring to the boil. Season to taste.
4 Spoon mixture into four 1¼-cup (310ml) ovenproof
dishes; sprinkle with topping. Bake about 20 minutes
or until browned lightly.

CRUMBLE OAT TOPPING Process ingredients until
coarsely chopped.

prep + cook time 45 minutes serves 4
nutritional count per serving 52g total fat
(32.5g saturated fat); 2909kJ (696 cal);
23g carbohydrate; 31.5g protein; 8.3g fibre

note We used larger dishes here – each dish will serve two.

salmon, potato and rocket cake

1kg (2 pounds) potatoes, chopped coarsely
1 cup (240g) light sour cream
½ cup (125ml) pouring cream
2 eggs, beaten lightly
250g (8 ounces) rocket (arugula), trimmed,
  chopped coarsely
¾ cup (60g) finely grated parmesan cheese
400g (12½ ounces) canned red salmon, drained, flaked

1 Preheat oven to 180°C/350°F.
2 Boil, steam or microwave potato until tender; drain. Mash potato in large bowl with sour cream and cream until smooth. Stir in egg, rocket and ½ cup (40g) of the cheese; season.
3 Divide half the mixture between four 1½-cup (375ml) ovenproof dishes; top with salmon. Cover salmon with remaining potato mixture; sprinkle with remaining cheese. Bake, uncovered, about 30 minutes or until browned lightly and set.

prep + cook time 1 hour 10 minutes **serves** 4
nutritional count per serving 43.2g total fat (23.3g saturated fat); 2784kJ (666 cal); 31.5g carbohydrate; 36g protein; 4.1g fibre

note We used sebago potatoes in this recipe.

jansson's temptation

80g (3 ounces) canned anchovies in oil
1 large brown onion (200g), sliced thinly
1kg (2 pounds) potatoes, sliced thinly
1 cup (250ml) pouring cream
2 tablespoons stale breadcrumbs
30g (1 ounce) butter, chopped finely

1   Preheat oven to 220°C/425°F.
2   Drain anchovies over medium frying pan; finely chop anchovies. Heat anchovy oil in pan; cook onion, stirring, until soft.

3   Layer one-third of potato over base of 1.5-litre (6-cup) ovenproof dish; sprinkle with one-third of the onion and anchovy. Repeat layering with remaining potato, onion and anchovy. Pour over cream; sprinkle with breadcrumbs. Dot with butter.
4   Cover dish loosely with foil; bake about 1 hour or until potato is tender. Uncover; bake about 15 minutes or until browned lightly.

prep + cook time 1 hour 40 minutes **serves** 4
nutritional count per serving 39.3g total fat
(22.9g saturated fat); 2224kJ (532 cal);
32.6g carbohydrate; 10.6g protein; 4g fibre

creamy fish and potato bake

3 cups (750ml) milk
3 cloves garlic, crushed
1kg (2 pounds) potatoes, sliced thinly
45g (1½ ounces) butter, chopped finely
2 medium brown onions (300g), sliced thinly
2 tablespoons plain (all-purpose) flour
500g (1 pound) skinless white fish fillets, sliced thickly

1 Preheat oven to 220°C/425°F.
2 Combine milk and garlic in large saucepan; bring almost to the boil. Season. Add potato; simmer, stirring occasionally, about 15 minutes or until potato is tender. Drain over large heatproof bowl; reserve milk mixture.
3 Melt butter in large frying pan; cook onion, stirring, until soft. Add flour; cook, stirring, about 2 minutes or until mixture bubbles and thickens. Gradually stir in reserved milk; cook, stirring, until mixture boils and thickens. Stir in potato.
4 Divide half the potato mixture into six 1-cup (250ml) shallow ovenproof dishes; top with fish, then remaining potato mixture. Bake, uncovered, about 15 minutes or until fish is cooked.

prep + cook time 50 minutes **serves** 6
nutritional count per serving 13.1g total fat (7.9g saturated fat); 1442kJ (345 cal); 29.3g carbohydrate; 25.7g protein; 3.2g fibre

notes A mandolin or V-slicer is ideal for thinly slicing potatoes. As you need the starch from the potatoes in this recipe, don't rinse them after slicing. To stop them turning brown, add them to the hot milk and garlic as soon as they are sliced. We used desiree potatoes in this recipe. Use any white fish fillets you like; we used blue-eye. We used two large dishes here – each will serve three.

spicy sardine and spaghetti bake

250g (8 ounces) spaghetti
1 cup (70g) stale breadcrumbs
⅓ cup finely chopped fresh flat-leaf parsley
⅓ cup (80ml) olive oil
318g (10 ounces) canned sardines in oil, drained
250g (8 ounces) cherry tomatoes, chopped coarsely
4 cloves garlic, crushed
1½ teaspoons dried chilli flakes

1 Preheat oven to 220°C/425°F.
2 Cook pasta in large saucepan of boiling water until tender; drain, reserve ⅓ cup (80ml) cooking liquid.
3 Combine breadcrumbs, parsley and 1 tablespoon of the oil in medium bowl.
4 Heat remaining oil in same pan; cook sardines, tomato, garlic and chilli, stirring, until tomato begins to soften. Stir in pasta; season to taste.
5 Spoon mixture into 2-litre (8-cup) ovenproof dish; pour over reserved cooking liquid. Sprinkle with breadcrumb mixture. Bake, uncovered, about 10 minutes or until browned lightly.

prep + cook time 30 minutes **serves** 4
nutritional count per serving 29.7g total fat
(6.1g saturated fat); 2500kJ (598 cal);
56.3g carbohydrate; 24g protein; 4.6g fibre

note Seasoning a dish with pepper when it already contains chilli isn't doubling up, as they both have distinct flavours.

prawns and fetta with crispy fillo

1 tablespoon olive oil
1 large brown onion (200g), chopped finely
1 medium red capsicum (bell pepper) (200g), sliced thinly
2 garlic cloves, crushed
1 cup (250g) bottled tomato pasta sauce
½ cup (125ml) water
½ teaspoon dried oregano
¼ teaspoon dried chilli flakes
1kg (2 pounds) uncooked medium king prawns (shrimp)
100g (3 ounces) soft fetta cheese, crumbled
8 sheets fillo pastry
45g (1½ ounces) butter, melted

1 Preheat oven to 220°C/425°F.
2 Heat oil in large frying pan; cook onion and capsicum, stirring, until onion softens. Add garlic; cook, stirring, until fragrant. Add sauce, the water, oregano and chilli; simmer, uncovered, until sauce thickens slightly. Season to taste.
3 Transfer tomato mixture to 1.5-litre (6-cup) ovenproof dish. Shell and devein prawns; stir into tomato mixture. Sprinkle with cheese; bake, uncovered, 10 minutes.
4 Meanwhile, stack four sheets of pastry, brushing with butter between each layer. Roll pastry stack loosely; cut roll into thick strips. Repeat with remaining pastry. Loosen pastry rolls with fingers; sprinkle randomly over prawn mixture. Bake, uncovered, about 15 minutes or until browned lightly.

prep + cook time 40 minutes serves 4
nutritional count per serving 21.2g total fat (10.2g saturated fat); 1868kJ (447 cal); 27.1g carbohydrate; 35.4g protein; 3.5g fibre

note We've used medium pans here – each pan will serve two. Use pans that have ovenproof handles, or wrap regular handles in several layers of foil to protect them from the heat of the oven.

smoked haddock potato bake

500g (1 pound) potatoes
70g (2½ ounces) butter
1 medium brown onion (150g), chopped finely
2 stalks celery (300g), trimmed, sliced thinly
2 tablespoons plain (all-purpose) flour
1 cup (250ml) fish stock
500g (1 pound) smoked haddock, skinned,
  chopped coarsely
1 cup (120g) frozen peas
½ cup (125ml) pouring cream
2 tablespoons coarsely chopped fresh flat-leaf parsley

1 Preheat oven to 220°C/425°F.
2 Boil, steam or microwave potatoes until almost tender; drain. When cool enough to handle, slice thinly.
3 Meanwhile, melt 50g (1½ ounces) of the butter in large saucepan; cook onion and celery, stirring, until onion softens. Add flour; cook, stirring, about 2 minutes or until mixture bubbles and thickens. Gradually stir in stock; cook, stirring, until mixture boils and thickens. Remove from heat; stir in fish, peas, cream and parsley. Season to taste.
4 Spoon mixture into shallow 1.5-litre (6-cup) ovenproof dish; top with potato. Brush with remaining melted butter. Bake, uncovered, about 25 minutes or until browned lightly.

prep + cook time 50 minutes serves 6
nutritional count per serving 19.7g total fat
(12.5g saturated fat); 1430kJ (342 cal);
15.6g carbohydrate; 24.1g protein; 3.6g fibre

notes We used desiree potatoes in this recipe.
Season this dish carefully as the haddock and stock
are already salty.

salmon bread and butter pudding

8 large slices white bread (500g), crusts removed
45g (1½ ounces) butter, softened
150g (4½ ounces) piece hot-smoked salmon, flaked
4 eggs
2 cups (500ml) milk
1 cup (250ml) pouring cream
2 tablespoons finely chopped fresh chives
2 teaspoons finely chopped fresh tarragon
1 tablespoon dijon mustard
½ cup (60g) coarsely grated cheddar cheese

1 Preheat oven to 200°C/400°F. Grease 2-litre (8-cup) ovenproof dish.
2 Spread both sides of bread with butter; cut into triangles. Layer bread, slightly overlapping, in dish; sprinkle with salmon.

3 Whisk eggs, milk, cream, chives, tarragon, mustard and half the cheese in medium bowl until combined; season. Pour half the egg mixture over bread. Stand 1 hour.
4 Pour remaining egg mixture into dish; sprinkle with remaining cheese. Place ovenproof dish in large baking dish. Add enough hot water to baking dish to come halfway up the sides of ovenproof dish. Cover loosely with foil; bake 25 minutes. Uncover; bake about 20 minutes or until set. Remove pudding from baking dish. Stand 5 minutes before serving.

prep + cook time 1 hour (+ standing) serves 4
nutritional count per serving 56.5g total fat
(32.8g saturated fat); 3800kJ (909 cal);
64.3g carbohydrate; 35.3g protein; 3.8g fibre

spicy tuna pasta bake

300g (9½ ounces) cannelloni tubes
2 tablespoons olive oil
3 cloves garlic, crushed
4 drained anchovy fillets, chopped finely
2 cups (500g) bottled tomato pasta sauce
½ cup (75g) seeded kalamata olives, halved
2 tablespoons finely chopped fresh oregano
1 tablespoon rinsed, drained capers
½ teaspoon dried chilli flakes
425g (13½ ounces) canned tuna in oil, drained, flaked
¼ cup (25g) coarsely grated mozzarella cheese
¼ cup (20g) finely grated parmesan cheese

1 Preheat oven to 220°C/425°F.
2 Cook pasta in large saucepan of boiling water until tender; drain, reserving ¼ cup (60ml) of cooking liquid.
3 Meanwhile, heat oil in large saucepan; cook garlic and anchovy, stirring, until fragrant. Stir in sauce, olives, oregano, capers and chilli; simmer, uncovered, 5 minutes. Season to taste. Stir in pasta, tuna and the reserved cooking liquid.
4 Spoon mixture into 2-litre (8-cup) ovenproof dish; sprinkle with combined cheeses. Bake, uncovered, about 15 minutes or until browned lightly.

prep + cook time 35 minutes **serves** 4
nutritional count per serving 26.5g total fat
(5.3g saturated fat); 2730kJ (653 cal);
66g carbohydrate; 34.6g protein; 6g fibre

sardine, potato and lemon bake

¼ cup (60ml) olive oil
1kg (2 pounds) potatoes, peeled, sliced thinly
1 tablespoon honey
1 tablespoon finely chopped preserved lemon rind
1 teaspoon harissa paste
10 fresh sardine fillets (375g)

1 Preheat oven to 220°C/425°F.
2 Heat oil in large frying pan; cook potato, in batches, stirring, about 10 minutes or until browned lightly. Drain oil from potato over medium heatproof bowl; stir honey, rind and harissa into bowl, season.
3 Layer potato and sardines in 1.5-litre (6-cup) ovenproof dish. Pour honey mixture into dish. Bake, uncovered, about 20 minutes or until sardines are cooked.

prep + cook time 40 minutes **serves** 4
nutritional count per serving 23.9g total fat
(4.6g saturated fat); 1898kJ (454 cal);
32.6g carbohydrate; 25.3g protein; 3.4g fibre

note A mandolin or V-slicer is ideal to quickly slice potatoes evenly. Rinse the sliced potato in cold water to remove the starch and avoid the slices sticking together during cooking. Drain slices, then pat dry with absorbent paper before cooking.

tuna and corn bake

200g (6½ ounces) rigatoni pasta
45g (1½ ounces) butter
1½ tablespoons plain (all-purpose) flour
2½ cups (625ml) hot milk
1½ cups (180g) coarsely grated cheddar cheese
420g (13½ ounces) canned corn kernels, drained
425g (13½ ounces) canned tuna in springwater,
   drained, flaked
1 cup (120g) frozen peas
2 green onions (scallions), chopped finely
2 tablespoons finely chopped fresh flat-leaf parsley
2 tablespoons lemon juice

1 Preheat oven to 220°C/425°F.
2 Cook pasta in large saucepan of boiling water until
tender; drain.
3 Meanwhile, melt butter in medium saucepan. Add
flour; cook, stirring, about 2 minutes or until mixture
bubbles and thickens. Gradually stir in milk; cook, stirring,
until sauce boils and thickens. Stir in pasta, ⅓ cup of the
cheese, corn, tuna, peas, onion, parsley and juice; season
to taste.
4 Spoon mixture into 2-litre (8-cup) ovenproof dish; sprinkle
with remaining cheese. Bake, uncovered, about 25 minutes
or until browned lightly.

prep + cook time 40 minutes **serves** 6
nutritional count per serving 22.8g total fat
(13.9g saturated fat); 2103kJ (503 cal);
41.2g carbohydrate; 31.2g protein; 4.5g fibre

This is a take on the Russian coulibiac salmon pie. It's important to season each element (rice, fish and silver beet). Choose a fish fillet approximately the same length as the dish, or buy a thicker piece and butterfly it. To check if the salmon is cooked, insert a knife through the centre of the pie and check its temperature on your wrist; it should feel hot.

salmon, silver beet and rice pie

¼ cup (60ml) olive oil
1 large brown onion (200g), chopped finely
1½ cups (300g) jasmine rice
2¼ cups (560ml) water
2 eggs
1kg (2 pounds) silver beet (swiss chard), trimmed
500g (1 pound) skinless salmon fillet
2 cloves garlic, crushed
⅓ cup (80ml) thickened (heavy) cream
1 sheet puff pastry

1   Heat 2 tablespoons of the oil in medium saucepan; cook onion, stirring, until soft. Add rice; stir to coat in onion mixture. Add the water; bring to the boil. Reduce heat to medium-low; cook, covered, about 13 minutes or until water is absorbed and rice is tender. Transfer rice mixture to baking-paper-lined oven tray to cool.
2   Meanwhile, boil eggs in small saucepan of water for 6 minutes. Drain; rinse under cold water. Shell and halve eggs.

3   Preheat oven to 220°C/425°F. Grease shallow 1.25-litre (5-cup) square ovenproof dish.
4   Heat large frying pan; cook silver beet, stirring, until wilted. Remove from pan. When cool enough to handle, squeeze excess liquid from silver beet; chop coarsely.
5   Season salmon. Heat remaining oil in same pan; cook salmon on both sides until browned. Remove from pan. Add silver beet and garlic to same pan; cook, stirring, until fragrant. Stir in cream; season to taste.
6   Spread half the rice in dish; cover with half the silver beet. Top with salmon; place eggs along centre of salmon, cover with remaining silver beet to form a slight dome; cover with remaining rice. Cut pastry to fit dish; cover with pastry, tucking edges inside dish. Bake, uncovered, about 30 minutes or until browned lightly.

prep + cook time 1 hour 10 minutes   serves 6
nutritional count per serving 28.7g total fat
(6.9g saturated fat); 2462kJ (589 cal);
53.7g carbohydrate; 26.8g protein; 4.5g fibre

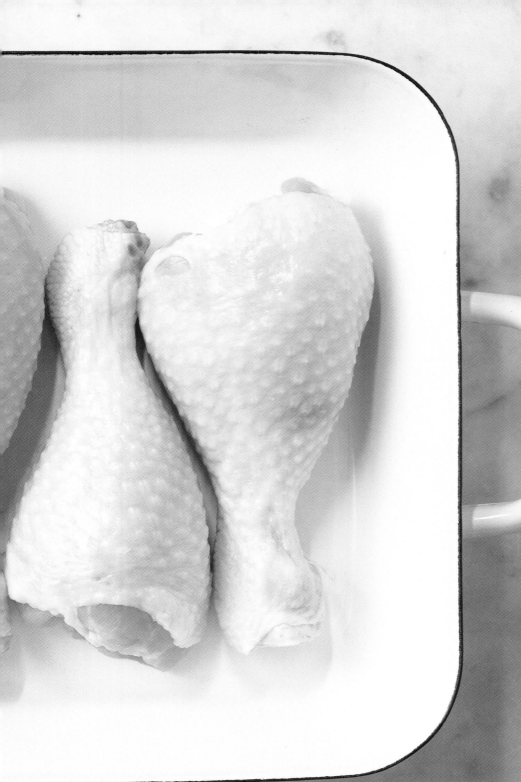

chicken

chicken and eggplant parmigiana

2 chicken breast fillets (400g)
2 tablespoons olive oil
1 medium eggplant (300g), sliced thinly
4 trimmed medium silver beet leaves (swiss chard) (320g)
1⅔ cups (400g) bottled tomato pasta sauce
1 cup (100g) coarsely grated mozzarella cheese
⅓ cup (25g) finely grated parmesan cheese

1 Preheat oven to 220°C/ 425°F.
2 Cut chicken breasts in half horizontally. Combine chicken and half the oil in large bowl. Cook chicken on heated oiled grill plate (or grill or barbecue) until browned both sides. Place in oiled 1.5-litre (6-cup) ovenproof dish.

3 Cook eggplant on heated oiled grill plate (or grill or barbecue), brushing with remaining oil, until browned and tender.
4 Meanwhile, boil, steam or microwave silver beet about 30 seconds or until just tender; transfer to bowl of iced water. Drain; squeeze excess water from silver beet. Drain on absorbent paper.
5 Top chicken with silver beet and eggplant, then sauce; sprinkle with combined cheeses. Bake, uncovered, about 20 minutes or until browned lightly.

prep + cook time 45 minutes **serves** 4
nutritional count per serving 20.2g total fat (6.7g saturated fat); 1555kJ (372 cal); 10.5g carbohydrate; 34.9g protein; 5.4g fibre

serving suggestion Serve with a green salad.

chicken, sausage and bean cassoulet

1kg (2 pounds) chicken pieces
½ cup (75g) plain (all-purpose) flour
¼ cup (60ml) olive oil
10 pork chipolata sausages (300g)
1 medium brown onion (150g), chopped coarsely
1 large carrot (180g), chopped coarsely
2 cloves garlic, sliced thinly
4 sprigs fresh thyme
1 bay leaf
2 tablespoons tomato paste
800g (1½ pounds) canned diced tomatoes
1 cup (250ml) chicken stock
840g (1¾ pounds) canned white beans, rinsed, drained
1 cup (70g) stale breadcrumbs
2 tablespoons finely chopped fresh flat-leaf parsley

1 Preheat oven to 200°C/400°F.
2 Coat chicken in flour; shake off excess. Heat half the oil in large flameproof casserole dish; cook chicken, in batches, until browned. Remove from dish.
3 Cook sausages, in same dish until browned. Remove from dish.
4 Heat remaining oil in same dish; cook onion, carrot, garlic, thyme and bay leaf, stirring, until onion softens. Add paste; cook, stirring, 1 minute. Return chicken and sausages to dish with undrained tomatoes and stock; bring to the boil. Cover; bake 20 minutes. Remove from oven; stir in beans. Cover; bake 30 minutes or until sauce thickens and chicken is tender. Season to taste. Preheat grill (broiler).
5 Sprinkle cassoulet with combined breadcrumbs and parsley; place under grill until browned lightly.

prep + cook time 1 hour 25 minutes serves 8
nutritional count per serving 26.2g total fat
(7.7g saturated fat); 1756kJ (420 cal);
21.6g carbohydrate; 22.6g protein; 5g fibre

chicken cacciatore with gremolata and parmesan topping

1.5kg (3 pounds) chicken pieces
⅓ cup (50g) plain (all-purpose) flour
2 tablespoons olive oil
1 large red onion (300g), chopped coarsely
2 cloves garlic, crushed
1 medium red capsicum (bell pepper) (200g), sliced thickly
½ cup (125ml) dry white wine
410g (13 ounces) canned diced tomatoes
410g (13 ounces) canned cherry tomatoes in tomato juice
½ cup (125ml) chicken stock
2 tablespoons tomato paste
1 teaspoon caster (superfine) sugar
½ cup (80g) seeded black olives

GREMOLATA AND PARMESAN TOPPING
½ cup (40g) coarsely grated parmesan cheese
⅓ cup finely chopped fresh flat-leaf parsley
1 tablespoon finely grated lemon rind
1 clove garlic, crushed

1 Preheat oven to 200°C/400°F.
2 Coat chicken in flour; shake off excess. Heat oil in large deep flameproof casserole dish; cook chicken, in batches, until browned. Remove from dish.
3 Cook onion, garlic and capsicum in same dish, stirring, until onion softens. Add wine; simmer, uncovered, until liquid is reduced by half. Stir in undrained tomatoes, stock, paste and sugar.
4 Return chicken to dish; bring to the boil. Cover; bake 45 minutes. Uncover; bake about 45 minutes or until chicken is tender and sauce has thickened. Skim fat from surface; stir in olives. Season to taste.
5 Meanwhile, make gremolata and parmesan topping. Sprinkle over dish just before serving.

GREMOLATA AND PARMESAN TOPPING Combine ingredients in a small bowl.

prep + cook time 1 hour 50 minutes serves 6
nutritional count per serving 29.1g total fat (8.6g saturated fat); 2019kJ (483 cal); 19g carbohydrate; 31.4g protein; 3.8g fibre

serving suggestion Serve with steamed rice or cooked pasta of your choice.

chicken and sweet corn bake

3 cups (480g) coarsely chopped barbecued chicken
420g (13½ ounces) canned creamed corn
1½ cup (180g) coarsely grated cheddar cheese
½ cup (125ml) pouring cream
4 green onions (scallions), sliced thinly
1 cup (70g) stale breadcrumbs

note You need to buy a large barbecued chicken to get the amount of shredded meat required for this recipe.

1 Preheat oven to 220°C/425°F.
2 Combine chicken, corn, cheese, cream and onion in large bowl; season. Spoon mixture into four oiled 1-cup (250ml) ovenproof dishes; sprinkle with breadcrumbs.
3 Place dishes on oven tray; bake about 20 minutes or until browned lightly.

prep + cook time 25 minutes **serves** 4
nutritional count per serving 26.9g total fat
(14.4g saturated fat); 2006kJ (480 cal);
27.2g carbohydrate; 30.4g protein; 5.1g fibre

cheesy chicken, tomato and bacon rigatoni

315g (10 ounces) rigatoni pasta
2 tablespoons olive oil
500g (1 pound) chicken tenderloins, sliced thinly
1 medium red onion (170g), sliced thinly
4 rindless bacon slices (260g), chopped coarsely
2 cups (500g) bottled tomato pasta sauce
¼ cup finely chopped fresh basil
1½ cups (180g) coarsely grated cheddar cheese

1 Preheat oven to 220°C/425°F.
2 Cook pasta in large saucepan of boiling water until tender; drain. Return to pan.
3 Meanwhile, heat half the oil in large frying pan; cook chicken until browned. Remove from pan.

4 Heat remaining oil in same pan; cook onion and bacon, stirring, until bacon is crisp. Return chicken to pan with sauce; simmer, uncovered, 10 minutes. Stir in basil; season.
5 Stir chicken mixture and half the cheese into pasta. Spoon pasta mixture into 2-litre (8-cup) ovenproof dish; sprinkle with remaining cheese. Bake, uncovered, about 15 minutes or until browned lightly.

prep + cook time 50 minutes serves 4
nutritional count per serving 34.9g total fat
(14g saturated fat); 3540kJ (847 cal);
65.8g carbohydrate; 64g protein; 6g fibre

mexican chicken tortilla bake

1 tablespoon olive oil
1 large red onion (300g), sliced thinly
1 medium red capsicum (bell pepper) (200g), sliced thinly
800g (1½ pounds) canned diced tomatoes
420g (13½ ounces) canned kidney beans, rinsed, drained
310g (10 ounces) canned corn kernels, rinsed, drained
35g (1 ounce) taco seasoning
2 cups (320g) shredded barbecued chicken
⅓ cup coarsely chopped fresh coriander (cilantro)
4 x 19cm (7½-inch) flour tortillas
¾ cup (75g) coarsely grated mozzarella cheese

1 Preheat oven to 220°C/425°F.
2 Heat oil in large saucepan; cook onion and capsicum, stirring, until tender. Add undrained tomatoes, beans, corn and seasoning; simmer, uncovered, about 10 minutes or until thickened slightly. Add chicken and coriander; cook, stirring, until hot. Season to taste.
3 Line base and sides of 20cm (8-inch) springform pan with foil or baking paper; place on oven tray. Line base of pan with a tortilla; top with one-third of the chicken mixture. Repeat layering with remaining tortillas and chicken mixture, finishing with a tortilla; sprinkle with cheese. Bake, uncovered, about 20 minutes until browned lightly. Stand 5 minutes before cutting.

prep + cook time 45 minutes **serves** 6
nutritional count per serving 13.2g total fat (3.9g saturated fat); 1572kJ (376 cal); 33.8g carbohydrate; 26.4g protein; 8.1g fibre

serving suggestion Serve with an avocado salad or guacamole.
note You need to buy half large barbecued chicken (450g) to get the amount of shredded meat required for this recipe.

spicy chicken and ratatouille pilaf

2 tablespoons olive oil
1 medium red onion (170g), chopped coarsely
3 cloves garlic, sliced thinly
4 medium tomatoes (600g), chopped coarsely
2 medium zucchini (240g), chopped coarsely
1 medium eggplant (300g), chopped coarsely
1 medium red capsicum (bell pepper) (200g), chopped coarsely
1 cup (250g) bottled tomato pasta sauce
500g (1 pound) chicken tenderloins, sliced thinly
1 fresh long red chilli, chopped finely
1 cup (200g) basmati rice
1½ cups (375ml) chicken stock
¼ cup loosely packed fresh basil leaves

1 Preheat oven to 200°C/400°F.
2 Combine all ingredients, except basil, in 2.5-litre (10-cup) ovenproof dish. Cover tightly with foil; bake 50 minutes, stirring occasionally, or until rice is tender.
3 Stand, covered, 10 minutes; season to taste. Serve sprinkled with basil.

prep + cook time 1 hour 10 minutes **serves** 4
nutritional count per serving 9g total fat (1.5g saturated fat); 1430kJ (342 cal); 36.9g carbohydrate; 25.2g protein; 5.3g fibre

tip Using a round or oval dish will help the rice to cook more evenly, square corners attract the heat from the oven, which can cause the rice in the corners to dry out.

chicken, zucchini and mushroom lasagne

⅓ cup (80ml) olive oil
1 medium brown onion (150g), chopped finely
2 cloves garlic, crushed
500g (1 pound) minced (ground) chicken
2 tablespoons tomato paste
410g (13 ounces) canned diced tomatoes
1 teaspoon caster (superfine) sugar
⅓ cup coarsely chopped fresh basil
3 medium zucchini (360g), sliced thinly
5 flat mushrooms (400g), sliced thinly
375g (12 ounces) fresh lasagne sheets
⅓ cup (25g) finely grated parmesan cheese

WHITE SAUCE
60g (2 ounces) butter
¼ cup (35g) plain (all-purpose) flour
2¼ cups (560ml) hot milk
⅓ cup (25g) finely grated parmesan cheese

1 Preheat oven to 200°C/400°F.
2 Heat 1 tablespoon of the oil in medium saucepan; cook onion and garlic, stirring, until onion softens. Add chicken; stir until browned. Add paste, undrained tomatoes and sugar; bring to the boil. Reduce heat; simmer, uncovered, 5 minutes. Stir in basil; season.

3 Cook zucchini and mushrooms, in batches, on heated oiled grill plate (or grill or barbecue), brushing with remaining oil, until browned and tender.
4 Meanwhile, make white sauce.
5 Line base of 2-litre (8-cup) ovenproof dish with lasagne sheets, trimming to fit. Top with one-third of the chicken mixture, half the vegetable mixture and half the white sauce. Top with lasagne sheets, trimming to fit. Top with half the remaining chicken mixture, remaining vegetable mixture, lasagne sheets, then remaining chicken mixture. Top with remaining lasagne sheets and remaining white sauce; sprinkle with cheese.
6 Cover dish with foil; bake 20 minutes. Uncover; bake about 30 minutes or until browned lightly. Stand 10 minutes before serving.

WHITE SAUCE Melt butter in medium saucepan. Add flour; cook, stirring, 2 minutes. Remove from heat; gradually stir in milk. Cook, stirring, until sauce boils and thickens. Simmer, uncovered, 3 minutes. Season to taste. Remove from heat; stir in cheese.

prep + cook time 1 hour 15 minutes serves 6
nutritional count per serving 34.8g total fat (13.4g saturated fat); 2909kJ (696 cal); 59.8g carbohydrate; 34.4g protein; 6.6g fibre

serving suggestion Serve with a mixed green salad.

red curry chicken risotto

1 tablespoon peanut oil
500g (1 pound) chicken thigh fillets, chopped coarsely
1 medium brown onion (150g), chopped finely
1 medium red capsicum (bell pepper) (200g),
  chopped coarsely
1 fresh long red chilli, sliced thinly
3 cloves garlic, crushed
1½ cups (300g) arborio rice
¼ cup (75g) red curry paste
2 cups (500ml) chicken stock
½ cup (125ml) water
4 kaffir lime leaves, sliced thinly
1 cup (250ml) coconut cream
125g (4 ounces) green beans, trimmed, halved
30g (1 ounce) baby spinach leaves, chopped coarsely
¼ cup loosely packed fresh coriander (cilantro) leaves

1 Preheat oven to 200°C/400°F.
2 Heat oil in large flameproof casserole dish; cook chicken until browned. Remove from dish.
3 Heat remaining oil in same dish; cook onion, capsicum, chilli and garlic, stirring, until onion softens. Add rice and paste; cook, stirring, 1 minute.
4 Return chicken to dish with stock, the water and lime leaves. Cover with foil; bake about 50 minutes, stirring occasionally, or until rice is tender. Remove from oven; stir in coconut cream, beans and spinach. Cover; stand 10 minutes. Season to taste; serve sprinkled with coriander.

prep + cook time 1 hour 15 minutes **serves** 4
nutritional count per serving 32.6g total fat
(15.4g saturated fat); 2980kJ (713 cal);
68.7g carbohydrate; 33.8g protein; 5.5g fibre

note Use whatever type of curry paste you prefer.

creamy chicken, bacon and corn chowder

45g (1½ ounces) butter
2 rindless bacon slices (130g), chopped finely
1 medium leek (350g), sliced thinly
2 stalks celery (300g), trimmed, chopped finely
1 medium carrot (120g), chopped finely
¼ cup (35g) plain (all-purpose) flour
2 cups (500ml) hot milk
½ cup (125ml) pouring cream
2 medium potatoes (400g), chopped coarsely
1 fresh bay leaf
2 chicken breast fillets (400g), chopped coarsely
310g (10 ounces) canned corn kernels, rinsed, drained
2 tablespoons finely chopped fresh chives
200g (6½ ounces) crusty bread, cut into small cubes

1 Preheat oven to 200°C/400°F.
2 Melt butter in large saucepan; cook bacon, leek, celery and carrot, stirring, until vegetables soften. Add flour; cook, stirring, 1 minute. Gradually stir in milk and cream; stir in potato and bay leaf. Cook, stirring, until mixture boils and thickens. Simmer, uncovered, about 5 minutes or until potato is tender. Stir in chicken, corn and chives.
3 Spoon mixture into 2-litre (8-cup) ovenproof dish; sprinkle with bread. Bake, uncovered, about 30 minutes or until browned lightly.

prep + cook time 1 hour **serves** 6
nutritional count per serving 21.8g total fat (12.5g saturated fat); 2073kJ (496 cal); 42.1g carbohydrate; 30g protein; 6.1g fibre

note Discard bay leaf before serving.

chicken biryani with cauliflower and peas

¼ cup (70g) yogurt
2 cups (540g) bottled butter chicken simmer sauce
500g (1 pound) chicken thigh fillets, trimmed,
  chopped coarsely
1½ cups (300g) basmati rice
2 tablespoons vegetable oil
2½ cups (250g) cauliflower florets
1 large brown onion (200g), sliced thinly
3 cloves garlic, crushed
2.5cm (1-inch) piece fresh ginger (15g), grated
1 fresh long green chilli, sliced thinly
1 tablespoon garam masala
4 cloves
2 teaspoons ground turmeric
3 cups (750ml) chicken stock
½ cup (60g) frozen peas, thawed
⅓ cup (55g) dried currants
¼ cup loosely packed fresh coriander (cilantro) leaves

1 Combine yogurt, ¼ cup of the simmer sauce and chicken in large bowl. Cover; refrigerate 1 hour.
2 Preheat oven to 200°C/400°F.
3 Rinse rice under cold water until water runs clear; drain. Heat half the oil in large flameproof casserole dish; cook cauliflower, stirring, about 5 minutes or until browned lightly and tender. Remove from pan.
4 Heat remaining oil in same dish; cook onion, stirring, until browned lightly. Add chicken; cook, stirring, until browned. Add garlic, ginger, chilli and spices; cook, stirring, about 1 minute or until fragrant. Add rice; cook, stirring, 1 minute. Stir in stock. Cover; bake about 45 minutes or until rice is tender and liquid absorbed.
5 Remove dish from oven; add cauliflower, peas and currants. Cover, stand for 10 minutes. Fluff rice with a fork; season to taste.
6 Bring remaining simmer sauce to the boil in small saucepan. Serve biryani topped with heated simmer sauce, coriander leaves and some extra yogurt, if you like.

prep + cook time 1 hour 15 minutes (+ refrigeration)
serves 4
nutritional count per serving 32.1g total fat
(9.9g saturated fat); 3260kJ (780 cal);
84.7g carbohydrate; 35.1g protein; 7.5g fibre

chicken stroganoff with potato topping

4 medium potatoes (800g), chopped coarsely
½ cup (125ml) milk
60g (2 ounces) butter
500g (1 pound) chicken thigh fillets, sliced thinly
¼ cup (35g) plain (all-purpose) flour
2 tablespoons olive oil
45g (1½ ounces) butter, extra
1 large brown onion (200g), sliced thinly
2 cloves garlic, crushed
185g (6 ounces) button mushrooms, sliced thinly
2 teaspoons sweet paprika
⅓ cup (80ml) dry white wine
1 cup (250ml) chicken stock
1 tablespoon worcestershire sauce
¼ cup (70g) tomato paste
½ cup (120g) light sour cream
2 tablespoons finely chopped fresh flat-leaf parsley

1 Preheat oven to 220°C/425°F.
2 Boil, steam or microwave potato until tender; drain. Mash potato with milk and butter in large bowl until smooth.
3 Meanwhile, coat chicken in flour; shake off excess. Heat oil in large saucepan; cook chicken until browned. Remove from pan.
4 Melt extra butter in same pan; cook onion, garlic and mushrooms, stirring, until vegetables soften. Add paprika; cook, stirring, about 1 minute or until fragrant. Add wine and stock; simmer, uncovered, until liquid is reduced by half. Return chicken to pan with sauce, paste and sour cream; bring to the boil. Remove from heat; stir in parsley. Season to taste.
5 Spoon chicken mixture into 2.5-litre (10-cup) ovenproof dish. Top with potato; roughen surface with a fork. Bake, uncovered, about 30 minutes or until browned lightly.

prep + cook time 1 hour serves 6
nutritional count per serving 31.7g total fat
(15.4g saturated fat); 2052kJ (491 cal);
24.9g carbohydrate; 22.8g protein; 3.9g fibre

red wine and rosemary chicken with polenta crust

8 chicken thigh fillets (1.6kg), halved
2 tablespoons plain (all-purpose) flour
1 teaspoon cracked black pepper
2 tablespoons olive oil
125g (4 ounces) speck, chopped coarsely
8 shallots (200g), halved
1 large carrot (180g), chopped coarsely
4 cloves garlic, sliced thinly
2 sprigs rosemary
1 cup (250ml) dry red wine
1 cup (250ml) chicken stock
2 tablespoons tomato paste
½ cup (50g) coarsely grated mozzarella cheese

POLENTA CRUST
1 cup (250ml) chicken stock
1 cup (250ml) milk
½ cup (85g) polenta

1 Preheat oven to 200°C/400°F.
2 Coat chicken in combined flour and pepper; shake off excess.
3 Heat oil in large frying pan; cook chicken, in batches, until browned. Remove from pan.
4 Cook speck, shallots, carrot and garlic in same pan, stirring, until browned lightly. Return chicken to pan with rosemary, wine, stock and paste; bring to the boil. Season. Spoon mixture into six 1-cup (250ml) ovenproof dishes; bake, covered, 20 minutes.
5 Meanwhile, make polenta crust.
6 Spread polenta crust mixture over chicken mixture; sprinkle with cheese. Bake, uncovered, about 20 minutes or until browned lightly. Stand 10 minutes before serving.

POLENTA CRUST Bring stock and milk to the boil in small saucepan; gradually stir in polenta. Reduce heat; simmer, stirring, about 10 minutes or until polenta thickens.

prep + cook time 1 hour 40 minutes serves 6
nutritional count per serving 34.7g total fat (11.9g saturated fat); 2972kJ (711 cal); 30.4g carbohydrate; 61.5g protein; 2.6g fibre

note If speck is unavailable, use three chopped bacon slices.

meat

lamb shank shepherd's pie

4 french-trimmed lamb shanks (1kg)
⅓ cup (50g) plain (all-purpose) flour
2 tablespoons olive oil
8 baby brown onions (200g), peeled
1 large carrot (180g), chopped coarsely
4 cloves garlic, sliced thinly
2 tablespoons each fresh thyme and rosemary leaves
½ cup (125ml) dry white wine
1¼ cups (310ml) chicken stock
1¼ cups (310ml) water
1kg (2 pounds) potatoes, chopped coarsely
45g (1½ ounces) butter
½ cup (125ml) hot milk

CREAMED SPINACH
1 tablespoon olive oil
30g (1 ounce) butter
1 small brown onion (80g), chopped finely
2 cloves garlic, crushed
1kg (2 pounds) spinach, trimmed
½ cup (125ml) pouring cream
pinch ground nutmeg

1 Preheat oven to 200°C/400°F.
2 Coat lamb in flour; shake off excess. Heat half the oil in large flameproof casserole dish; cook lamb until browned. Remove from dish.
3 Heat remaining oil in same dish; cook onions, carrot, garlic and herbs, stirring, until onions are browned lightly. Add wine; boil, uncovered, until liquid is evaporated. Return lamb to dish with stock and the water; bring to the boil. Cover dish tightly with foil; bake about 2 hours or until lamb is tender.
4 Meanwhile, boil, steam or microwave potato until tender; drain. Mash potato in medium bowl with butter and hot milk until smooth. Season to taste. Make creamed spinach.
5 Remove dish from oven; discard lamb shank bones. Break meat into large chunks; return meat to dish. Combine potato and spinach in large bowl; spoon over lamb mixture. Bake, uncovered, about 30 minutes or until browned lightly.

CREAMED SPINACH Heat oil and butter in large frying pan; cook onion and garlic, stirring, until onion softens. Add spinach, in batches, stirring, until wilted and liquid is evaporated. Add cream and nutmeg; simmer about 3 minutes or until thickened slightly. Season to taste.

prep + cook time 2 hours 50 minutes serves 6
nutritional count per serving 38.4g total fat
(18.4g saturated fat); 2575kJ (616 cal);
30.8g carbohydrate; 29.5g protein; 8.8g fibre

beef stew with chive dumplings

1kg (2 pounds) beef chuck steak, chopped coarsely
2 tablespoons plain (all-purpose) flour
2 tablespoons olive oil
15g (½ ounce) butter
1 medium brown onion (150g), chopped coarsely
2 cloves garlic, crushed
1 medium parsnip (250g), chopped coarsely
1 medium carrot (120g), chopped coarsely
1 cup (250ml) dry red wine
1½ cups (375ml) beef stock
2 tablespoons tomato paste
4 sprigs fresh thyme

CHIVE DUMPLINGS
1 cup (150g) self-raising flour
60g (2 ounces) butter, chopped finely
1 egg, beaten lightly
¼ cup (20g) coarsely grated parmesan cheese
¼ cup finely chopped fresh chives
¼ cup (60ml) milk, approximately

1 Preheat oven to 180°C/350°F.
2 Coat beef in flour; shake off excess. Heat oil in large flameproof baking dish; cook beef, in batches, until browned. Remove from dish.
3 Melt butter in same dish; cook onion, garlic, parsnip and carrot, stirring, until onion softens. Add wine; cook, stirring, until liquid reduces by half. Return beef to dish with stock, paste and thyme; bring to the boil. Season. Cover; bake 1¾ hours.
4 Meanwhile, make chive dumplings.
5 Remove dish from oven. Drop rounded tablespoons of dumpling mixture, about 2cm (¾ inch) apart, on top of stew. Bake, uncovered, about 25 minutes or until dumplings are browned lightly.

CHIVE DUMPLINGS Place flour in medium bowl; rub in butter. Stir in egg, cheese, chives and enough milk to make a soft sticky dough.

prep + cook time 2 hours 20 minutes serves 4
nutritional count per serving 47.7g total fat
(19.7g saturated fat); 3837kJ (918 cal);
42.3g carbohydrate; 67.5g protein; 5.1g fibre

baked meatballs

1kg (2 pounds) minced (ground) beef
2 eggs
1 cup (100g) packaged breadcrumbs
½ cup (40g) finely grated parmesan cheese
⅓ cup finely chopped fresh flat-leaf parsley
¼ cup (60ml) olive oil
1 medium brown onion (150g), chopped finely
2 cloves garlic, crushed
2⅔ cups (700g) bottled tomato pasta sauce
800g (1½ pounds) canned crushed tomatoes
1 cup (120g) frozen peas
½ cup coarsely chopped fresh basil
200g (6½ ounces) ricotta cheese
½ cup (40g) finely grated parmesan cheese, extra

1 Preheat oven to 200°C/400°F. Oil 3-litre (12-cup) ovenproof dish.
2 Combine beef, eggs, breadcrumbs, parmesan and parsley in large bowl; season. Using wet hands, roll rounded tablespoons of mixture into balls.
3 Heat half the oil in large frying pan; cook meatballs, in batches, until browned all over. Transfer to dish.
4 Heat remaining oil in same pan; cook onion and garlic, stirring, until onion softens. Remove from heat; stir in sauce, undrained tomatoes, peas and basil; season. Pour tomato mixture over meatballs; top with crumbled ricotta and extra parmesan. Bake, uncovered, about 40 minutes or until meatballs are cooked through.

prep + cook time 1 hour 10 minutes **serves** 6
nutritional count per serving 34.3g total fat (13.4g saturated fat); 2642kJ (632 cal); 27.3g carbohydrate; 50.9g protein; 7.1g fibre

serving suggestion Serve with pasta or crusty bread and a green salad.

osso bucco with polenta crust

8 pieces veal osso bucco (1.4kg)
⅓ cup (50g) plain (all-purpose) flour
2 tablespoons olive oil
30g (1 ounce) butter
1 large brown onion (200g), chopped finely
1 large carrot (180g), chopped finely
1 stalk celery (150g), chopped finely
4 cloves garlic, crushed
½ cup (125ml) dry white wine
800g (1½ pounds) canned crushed tomatoes
2 sprigs fresh rosemary
1 cup (250ml) chicken stock
1 tablespoon finely chopped fresh flat-leaf parsley
2 teaspoons finely grated lemon rind

POLENTA CRUST
2 cups (500ml) milk
2 cups (500ml) water
1 cup (150g) instant polenta
½ cup (40g) finely grated parmesan cheese
1 egg, beaten lightly

1 Preheat oven to 200°C/400°F.
2 Coat veal in flour; shake off excess. Heat half the oil and butter in large flameproof baking dish; cook veal, in batches, until browned. Remove from dish.
3 Heat remaining oil and butter in same dish; cook onion, carrot, celery and garlic, stirring, until onion softens. Add wine; boil, uncovered, until liquid has evaporated. Return veal to dish with undrained tomatoes, rosemary and stock; bring to the boil. Season. Cover tightly with foil; bake 1½ hours.
4 Meanwhile, make polenta crust.
5 Remove dish from oven; discard veal bones and rosemary. Break meat into large chunks. Divide veal mixture among eight oiled 1¼-cup (310ml) ovenproof dishes; top with polenta crust mixture. Place dishes on oven tray; bake, uncovered, about 25 minutes or until browned lightly. Serve sprinkled with combined parsley and rind.

POLENTA CRUST Combine milk and the water in medium saucepan; bring almost to the boil. Gradually stir in polenta, cook, stirring, about 5 minutes or until thickened. Remove from heat, stir in cheese and egg; season to taste.

prep + cook time 2 hours 20 minutes serves 8
nutritional count per serving 15.3g total fat
(6.3g saturated fat); 1705kJ (408 cal);
26.7g carbohydrate; 36.5g protein; 3.4g fibre

note We used larger dishes here – each will serve four.

salami antipasto pasta

375g (12 ounces) large shell pasta
200g (6½ ounces) shaved salami, chopped coarsely
⅓ cup (20g) drained semi-dried tomatoes
280g (9 ounces) bottled char-grilled vegetables, drained,
  chopped coarsely
2⅔ cups (700g) bottled tomato pasta sauce
2 cups (500ml) water
⅓ cup each coarsely chopped fresh basil and
  flat-leaf parsley
1 cup (100g) coarsely grated mozzarella cheese

1 Preheat oven to 200°C/400°F. Oil 2.5-litre (10-cup)
baking dish.
2 Combine pasta, salami, tomatoes, vegetables, sauce,
the water and chopped herbs in dish; season lightly.
3 Cover dish with foil; bake 50 minutes, stirring halfway
through cooking. Remove from oven; sprinkle with cheese.
Bake, uncovered, about 20 minutes or until pasta is tender.

prep + cook time 1 hour 20 minutes serves 6
nutritional count per serving 19.5g total fat
(6.8g saturated fat); 2098kJ (502 cal);
57.5g carbohydrate; 21.3g protein; 5.7g fibre

notes We have deliberately used dried, uncooked pasta
in this dish. The texture of the final dish is a little chewy,
but still tender.
We cooked this recipe in two ovenproof dishes – each
dish will serve three.

veal goulash with parsley dumplings

2 tablespoons olive oil
45g (1½ ounces) butter
1kg (2 pounds) veal shoulder, chopped coarsely
1 large red capsicum (bell pepper) (350g),
  chopped coarsely
1 large brown onion (200g), chopped coarsely
2 cloves garlic, crushed
2 tablespoons tomato paste
1 tablespoon plain (all-purpose) flour
1 tablespoon sweet paprika
2 teaspoons caraway seeds
½ teaspoon cayenne pepper
1½ cups (375ml) beef stock
½ cup (125ml) water
2 tablespoons coarsely chopped fresh flat-leaf parsley
¼ cup (20g) finely grated parmesan cheese

PARSLEY DUMPLINGS
1 cup (150g) self-raising flour
60g (2 ounces) butter, chopped finely
1 egg, beaten lightly
⅓ cup finely chopped fresh flat-leaf parsley
¼ cup (20g) finely grated parmesan cheese
¼ cup (60ml) milk, approximately

1 Preheat oven to 180°C/350°F.
2 Heat half the oil and butter in large flameproof casserole dish; cook veal, in batches, until browned. Remove from dish.
3 Heat remaining oil and butter in same dish; cook capsicum, onion and garlic, stirring, until vegetables soften. Add paste, flour, paprika, caraway and cayenne; cook, stirring, 1 minute. Return veal to dish with stock and the water; bring to the boil. Cover; bake 1½ hours.
4 Meanwhile, make parsley dumplings.
5 Remove dish from oven; stir in parsley. Season to taste. Drop rounded tablespoons of the dumpling mixture, about 2cm (¾ inch) apart, on top of goulash; sprinkle dumplings with cheese. Bake, uncovered, about 20 minutes or until dumplings are cooked through.

PARSLEY DUMPLINGS Place flour in medium bowl; rub in butter. Stir in egg, parsley, cheese and enough milk to make a soft sticky dough.

prep + cook time 2 hours 20 minutes serves 4
nutritional count per serving 42.7g total fat
(20.2g saturated fat); 3344kJ (800 cal);
35.7g carbohydrate; 67g protein; 3.7g fibre

pork sausage cassoulet

2 teaspoons olive oil
8 thick pork sausages (960g)
1 large brown onion (200g), chopped finely
155g (5 ounces) piece pancetta, chopped finely
1 medium carrot (120g), chopped coarsely
1 stalk celery (150g), trimmed, chopped coarsely
2 cloves garlic, crushed
2 tablespoons tomato paste
1½ cups (375ml) chicken stock
410g (13 ounces) canned crushed tomatoes
1 teaspoon fennel seeds
400g (12½ ounces) canned white beans, rinsed, drained
2 thick slices (100g) sourdough bread
1 tablespoon coarsely chopped fresh flat-leaf parsley

1 Preheat oven to 200°C/400°F.
2 Heat oil in large flameproof casserole dish; cook sausages, until browned. Drain sausages on absorbent paper, chop coarsely.
3 Cook onion, pancetta, carrot, celery and garlic in same dish, stirring, until onion softens. Add paste; cook, stirring, 1 minute. Return sausages to dish with stock, undrained tomatoes, fennel seeds and beans; bring to the boil. Bake, uncovered, 30 minutes.
4 Preheat grill (broiler). Season cassoulet to taste. Top with chunks of sourdough; grill until browned lightly. Sprinkle with parsley.

prep + cook time 1 hour 10 minutes serves 6
nutritional count per serving 41.6g total fat
(16.2g saturated fat); 2416kJ (578 cal);
20.2g carbohydrate; 28.8g protein; 6.2g fibre

egg and bacon pie

5 sheets fillo pastry
45g (1½ ounces) butter, melted
4 rindless bacon slices (260g), chopped finely
6 eggs
⅔ cup (160ml) milk
¾ cup (90g) coarsely grated cheddar cheese

1 Preheat oven to 200°C/400°F. Oil 20cm (8-inch) springform tin; place on oven tray.
2 Brush one sheet of fillo pastry with some of the melted butter; fold in half, then ease into base and side of tin. Repeat with remaining pastry and melted butter, to completely cover base and side of tin.
3 Cook bacon in heated oiled frying pan until crisp; drain on absorbent paper. Combine eggs and milk in large jug; season.
4 Place bacon and half the cheese in tin; pour in egg mixture. Sprinkle with remaining cheese. Roll down edges of pastry until touching egg mixture; bake, uncovered, about 45 minutes or until set. Stand 10 minutes before serving.

prep + cook time 1 hour 10 minutes serves 4
nutritional count per serving 32.5g total fat (16.6g saturated fat); 1965kJ (470 cal); 12.4g carbohydrate; 32.5g protein; 0.7g fibre

chorizo and chickpea stew

2 tablespoons olive oil
2 cured chorizo sausages (340g), sliced thickly
2 medium brown onions (300g), sliced thinly
1 tablespoon light brown sugar
2 teaspoons cumin seeds
1 teaspoon ground coriander
800g (1½ pounds) canned crushed tomatoes
800g (1½ pounds) canned chickpeas (garbanzos),
  rinsed, drained
1 cup (250ml) salt-reduced chicken stock
½ cup (75g) raisins
60g (2 ounces) baby spinach leaves

1 Preheat oven to 200°C/400°F.
2 Heat half the oil in large baking dish; cook chorizo,
stirring, until browned. Remove from dish. Add onion
and sugar to same dish; cook, stirring occasionally, over
medium heat, about 15 minutes or until onion is lightly
caramelised. Add spices; cook, stirring, 1 minute.
3 Return chorizo to dish with undrained tomatoes,
chickpeas, stock and raisins; bring to the boil. Cover;
bake 40 minutes. Remove from oven; stir in spinach.
Season to taste.

prep and cook time 1 hour 10 minutes serves 6
nutritional count per serving 25.5g total fat
(7.4g saturated fat); 1852kJ (443 cal);
31.8g carbohydrate; 19.3g protein; 7.5g fibre

beef ragu cannelloni

2 tablespoons olive oil
1 stalk celery (150g), trimmed, chopped finely
1 small brown onion (80g), chopped finely
1 small carrot (80g), chopped finely
2 fresh long red chillies, chopped finely
1 clove garlic, crushed
45g (1½ ounce) piece pancetta, chopped finely
250g (8 ounces) minced (ground) beef
200g (6½ ounces) minced (ground) pork
⅓ cup (80ml) dry white wine
¾ cup (180ml) milk
1 cup (250ml) chicken stock
410g (13 ounces) canned diced tomatoes
2 tablespoons tomato paste
2⅓ cups (580ml) thickened (heavy) cream
¾ cup (60g) finely grated parmesan cheese
250g (8 ounces) fresh cannelloni sheets

1 Heat half the oil in medium saucepan; cook celery, onion, carrot, chilli and garlic, stirring, until onion softens. Add pancetta; cook, stirring, 3 minutes. Remove from pan.
2 Heat remaining oil in same pan; cook beef and pork, stirring, until browned. Return pancetta mixture to pan with wine; boil, uncovered, until reduced by half. Add milk; bring to the boil. Boil, uncovered, until reduced by half. Add stock, undrained tomatoes and paste; bring to the boil. Reduce heat; simmer, uncovered, about 1 hour 10 minutes or until thickened. Season to taste. Cool 20 minutes.
3 Preheat oven to 200°C/400°F. Oil shallow 3.5-litre (14-cup) ovenproof dish.
4 Combine cream and cheese in large jug; season. Spread 1 cup of the cream mixture over base of dish.
5 Carefully tear each cannelloni sheet into three pieces. Place ¼ cup of beef mixture along one short side of each piece; roll to enclose. Place cannelloni, seam-side down, into dish; pour remaining cream mixture over cannelloni. Cover with foil; bake 30 minutes. Uncover; bake about 15 minutes or until browned lightly. Stand 5 minutes before serving.

prep + cook time 2 hours 15 minutes (+ cooling) serves 6
nutritional count per serving 54.3g total fat
(30.3g saturated fat); 3097kJ (741 cal);
31.7g carbohydrate; 28.9g protein; 3.4g fibre

sweet and sour meatballs

1kg (2 pounds) minced (ground) beef
2 eggs
1 cup (100g) packaged breadcrumbs
1 tablespoon finely chopped fresh flat-leaf parsley
¼ cup (60ml) olive oil
1 large red capsicum (bell pepper) (350g),
  chopped coarsely
1 large brown onion (200g), chopped coarsely
1 large carrot (180g), chopped coarsely
2 stalks celery (300g), trimmed, chopped coarsely

SWEET AND SOUR SAUCE
440g (14 ounces) canned pineapple pieces in natural juice
2 tablespoons cornflour (cornstarch)
2 tablespoons light soy sauce
¾ cup (180ml) water
⅔ cup (160ml) white vinegar
⅓ cup (80ml) tomato sauce (ketchup)
3 teaspoons caster (superfine) sugar

1   Preheat oven to 200°C/400°F. Oil 3-litre (12-cup) ovenproof dish.
2   Make sweet and sour sauce.
3   Combine beef, eggs, breadcrumbs and parsley in large bowl; season. Using wet hands, roll rounded tablespoons of beef mixture into balls.
4   Heat half the oil in large frying pan; cook meatballs, in batches, until browned. Transfer to dish. Heat remaining oil in same pan; cook capsicum, onion, carrot and celery, stirring, until onion softens. Add sweet and sour sauce; bring to the boil. Remove from heat; stir in reserved pineapple pieces.
5   Pour vegetable mixture over meatballs in dish. Cover dish with foil; bake 30 minutes. Uncover; bake about 10 minutes or until meatballs are cooked.

SWEET AND SOUR SAUCE Drain pineapple through sieve into large jug; reserve juice. Blend cornflour with soy sauce in medium jug; add juice, the water, vinegar, tomato sauce and sugar. Season.

prep + cook time 1 hour serves 6
nutritional count per serving 24.1g total fat
(8.1g saturated fat); 2149kJ (514 cal);
31.9g carbohydrate; 39.8g protein; 3.9g fibre

serving suggestion Serve with steamed jasmine rice.

lamb and eggplant pot pies with fetta crust

2 tablespoons olive oil
1 large eggplant (450g), peeled, chopped coarsely
1 large brown onion (200g), chopped finely
4 cloves garlic, crushed
1kg (2 pounds) minced (ground) lamb
1 teaspoon ground cinnamon
½ teaspoon ground allspice
1½ cups (375ml) beef stock
2 tablespoons tomato paste
¼ cup (20g) finely grated parmesan cheese
2 tablespoons each finely chopped fresh mint
 and oregano

FETTA CRUST
750g (1½ pounds) potatoes, chopped coarsely
30g (1 ounce) butter
¼ cup (60ml) hot milk
200g (6½ ounces) fetta cheese, crumbled

1   Heat half the oil in large saucepan; cook eggplant, stirring, until tender. Remove from pan. Heat remaining oil in same pan; cook onion and garlic, stirring, until onion softens. Add lamb; cook, stirring, until browned. Add spices; cook, stirring, 1 minute. Add stock and paste; bring to the boil. Reduce heat; simmer, uncovered, about 20 minutes or until thickened slightly. Remove from heat; stir in parmesan, herbs and eggplant.
2   Meanwhile, make fetta crust.
3   Preheat oven to 200°C/400°F. Oil six 1-cup (250ml) ovenproof dishes; place on oven trays.
4   Divide lamb mixture among dishes; top with fetta crust. Bake, uncovered, about 30 minutes or until browned lightly.

FETTA CRUST Boil, steam or microwave potato until tender; drain. Mash potato in medium bowl with butter and milk until smooth. Stir in fetta; season to taste.

prep and cook time 1 hour 10 minutes serves 6
nutritional count per serving 32.3g total fat
(15.3g saturated fat); 2341kJ (560 cal);
19g carbohydrate; 46.4g protein; 4.5g fibre

sausage risotto

1 tablespoon olive oil
6 thick beef sausages (900g)
1 medium brown onion (150g), chopped finely
¼ cup firmly packed fresh basil leaves
2 cloves garlic, crushed
2 cups (400g) arborio rice
2 tablespoons tomato paste
½ cup (125ml) dry white wine
2⅔ cups (700g) bottled tomato pasta sauce
2½ cups (625ml) water
2 teaspoons caster (superfine) sugar
60g (2 ounces) baby rocket (arugula) leaves

1 Preheat oven to 1
2 Heat oil in large fl.
sausages, in batches, ι   ...'
cut into thirds.
3 Cook onion, basil an   .. ιn same dish, stirring,
until onion softens. Add rice and paste; stir to coat rice
in onion mixture. Add wine; bring to the boil. Boil,
uncovered, stirring until liquid is absorbed. Stir in sauce,
the water and sugar; bring to the boil. Season.
4 Cover dish with foil; bake 25 minutes, stirring halfway
through cooking. Uncover; stir in sausages. Bake about
10 minutes or until rice is tender. Stir in rocket.

prep + cook time 1 hour serves 6
nutritional count per serving 43.5g total fat
(18.9g saturated fat); 3298kJ (789 cal);
68.7g carbohydrate; 24.6g protein; 8g fibre

glossary

ALLSPICE also calle
or pimento; taste
nutmeg, cumi
whole or
BAK

...d jamaican pepper ...like a combination of ...clove and cinnamon. Sold ...round.

...NG PAPER also known as parchment ...per or baking parchment; a silicone-coated paper that is used for lining baking pans and oven trays so cakes and biscuits won't stick, making removal easy.

BALSAMIC VINEGAR made from the juice of Trebbiano grapes; has a deep rich brown colour and a sweet and sour flavour.

BEAN SPROUTS tender new growths of assorted beans and seeds germinated for consumption as sprouts.

BEANS
broad also called fava, windsor and horse beans; available dried, fresh, canned and frozen. Fresh should be peeled twice (discarding both the outer long green pod and the beige-green tough inner shell); the frozen beans have had their pods removed but the beige shell still needs removal.
kidney medium-size red bean, slightly floury in texture yet sweet in flavour; sold dried or canned, it's found in bean mixes and is used in chilli con carne.
white a generic term we use for canned or dried cannellini, haricot, navy or great northern beans, all of which can be substituted for each other.

BREADCRUMBS
fresh bread, usually white, processed into crumbs.
japanese also called panko; available in two kinds: larger pieces and fine crumbs; they have a lighter texture than Western-style breadcrumbs. Available from Asian food stores and some supermarkets.
packaged prepared fine-textured but crunchy white breadcrumbs; good for coating foods that are to be fried.
stale crumbs made by grating or processing one- or two-day-old bread.

CAPERS the grey-green buds of a warm climate (usually Mediterranean) shrub, sold either dried and salted or pickled in a vinegar brine; tiny young ones, called baby capers, are also available both in brine or dried in salt. All capers should be rinsed before using.

CAPSICUM also called pepper or bell pepper. Discard seeds and membranes before use.

CARAWAY SEEDS small dried seed from a member of the parsley family; has a sharp anise flavour.

CAYENNE PEPPER a thin-fleshed, long, extremely hot dried red chilli, usually purchased ground.

CHEESE
blue mould-treated cheeses mottled with blue veining. Varieties include firm and crumbly stilton types and mild, creamy brie-like cheeses.
cheddar semi-hard, yellow to off-white, sharp-tasting cheese.
fetta Greek in origin; a crumbly textured goat- or sheep-milk cheese having a sharp, salty taste. Ripened and stored in salted whey; particularly good cubed and tossed into salads.
gorgonzola a creamy Italian blue cheese with a mild, sweet taste; good as an accompaniment to fruit or used to flavour sauces (especially pasta).
gruyère a hard-rind Swiss cheese with small holes and a nutty, slightly salty flavour. Popular for soufflés.
mozzarella soft, spun-curd cheese; originating in southern Italy where it was traditionally made from water-buffalo milk. Now generally made from cow's milk, it's a popular pizza cheese because of its low melting point and elasticity when heated.
parmesan also known as parmigiano, parmesan is a hard, grainy cow's-milk cheese that originated in the Parma region of Italy. The curd is salted in brine for a month before being aged for up to two years in humid conditions.
pizza cheese a commercial blend of varying proportions of processed grated mozzarella, cheddar and parmesan.

ricotta a soft, sweet, moist, white cow's-milk cheese with a low fat content (8.5%) and a slightly grainy texture. The name roughly translates as 'cooked again' and refers to ricotta's manufacture from a whey that is itself a by-product of cheese making.

CHICKPEAS also called garbanzos, hummus or channa; an irregularly round, sandy-coloured legume. Has a firm texture even after cooking, a floury mouth-feel and robust nutty flavour; available canned or dried (reconstitute for several hours in water before use).

CHIPOLATA SAUSAGES also known as 'little fingers'; highly spiced, coarse-textured beef sausage.

CHORIZO SAUSAGE of Spanish origin, made of coarsely ground pork and highly seasoned with garlic and chilli. They are deeply smoked, very spicy and dry-cured. Also available raw (fresh).

COCONUT
cream obtained commercially from the first pressing of the coconut flesh alone, without the addition of water.
milk not the liquid found inside the fruit, which is called coconut water, but the diluted liquid from the second pressing of the white flesh of a mature coconut (the first pressing produces coconut cream).

CORIANDER also called cilantro, pak chee or chinese parsley; bright-green-leafed herb with both pungent aroma and taste. Used as an ingredient in a wide variety of cuisines. Coriander seeds are dried and sold either whole or ground, and neither form tastes remotely like the fresh leaf, so should not be substituted.

CORNFLOUR also known as cornstarch. Available made from wheat (wheaten cornflour gives a lighter texture in cakes), or 100% corn (maize); used as a thickening agent in cooking.

CREAM we use fresh cream, also known as pure or pouring cream, unless otherwise stated. Has no additives. Minimum fat content 35%.

sour a thick, commercially cultured sour cream with a minimum fat content of 35%; light sour cream has 18.5% fat.

thick (double) a dolloping cream with a minimum fat content of 45%.

thickened (heavy) a whipping cream containing a thickener. Minimum fat content 35%.

CUMIN also known as zeera or comino; resembling caraway in size, cumin is the dried seed of a plant related to the parsley family. Its spicy, almost curry-like flavour is essential to the traditional foods of Mexico, India, North Africa and the Middle East. Also available ground.

DIJON MUSTARD also called french mustard. A pale brown, creamy, fairly mild mustard.

DRIED CURRANTS tiny, almost black raisins so-named after a grape variety that originated in Corinth, Greece.

EGGPLANT also called aubergine. Ranging in size from tiny to very large and in colour from pale green to deep purple. Can also be purchased char-grilled, packed in oil, in jars.

EGGS we use large chicken eggs weighing an average of 60g unless stated otherwise in the recipes in this book. If a recipe calls for raw or barely cooked eggs, exercise caution if there is a salmonella problem in your area, particularly in food eaten by children and pregnant women.

FENNEL also called finocchio or anise; a crunchy green vegetable slightly resembling celery that's eaten raw in salads, fried as an accompaniment, or used as an ingredient in soups and sauces. Also the name given to the dried seeds of the plant, which have a stronger licorice flavour.

FLOUR
plain also known as all-purpose; unbleached wheat flour is the best for baking: the gluten content ensures a strong dough, producing a light result.

self-raising all-purpose plain or wholemeal flour with baking powder and salt added; make yourself with plain flour sifted with baking powder in the proportion of 1 cup flour to 2 teaspoons baking powder.

GARAM MASALA literally meaning blended spices in its northern Indian place of origin; based on varying proportions of cardamom, cinnamon, cloves, coriander, fennel and cumin, roasted and ground together. Black pepper and chilli can be added.

GREEN ONION also known as scallion or, incorrectly, shallot; an immature onion picked before the bulb has formed, with a long, bright-green edible stalk.

HARISSA a North African paste made from dried red chillies, garlic, olive oil and caraway seeds; can be used as a rub for meat, an ingredient in sauces and dressings, or eaten as a condiment. It is available from Middle Eastern food shops and some supermarkets.

HORSERADISH a vegetable with edible green leaves but mainly grown for its long, pungent white root. Occasionally found fresh in specialty greengrocers and some Asian food shops, but commonly purchased in bottles at the supermarket in two forms: prepared horseradish and horseradish cream. These cannot be substituted one for the other in cooking but both can be used as table condiments. Horseradish cream is a commercially prepared creamy paste consisting of grated horseradish, vinegar, oil and sugar, while prepared horseradish is preserved grated root.

KAFFIR LIME LEAVES also known as bai magrood and looks like two glossy dark green leaves joined end to end, forming a rounded hourglass shape. Sold fresh, dried or frozen, the dried leaves are less potent so double the number if using them as a substitute for fresh; a strip of fresh lime peel may be substituted for each kaffir lime leaf.

KECAP MANIS a dark, thick sweet soy sauce used in most South-East Asian cuisines. Depending on the manufacturer, the sauce's sweetness is derived from the addition of either molasses or palm sugar when brewed.

KUMARA the Polynesian name of an orange-fleshed sweet potato often confused with yam.

LEEKS a member of the onion family, the leek resembles a green onion but is much larger and more subtle in flavour. Tender baby or pencil leeks can be eaten whole with minimal cooking but adult leeks are usually trimmed of most of the green tops then chopped or sliced and cooked.

MARINARA MIX a mixture of uncooked, chopped seafood available from many major supermarkets, as well as fishmarkets and fishmongers.

MUSHROOMS
button small, cultivated white mushrooms with a mild flavour. When a recipe calls for an unspecified type of mushroom, use button.
flat large, flat mushrooms with a rich earthy flavour, ideal for filling and barbecuing. They are sometimes misnamed field mushrooms, which are wild mushrooms.
swiss brown also known as roman or cremini. Light to dark brown mushrooms with full-bodied flavour; suited for use in casseroles or being stuffed and baked.

MUSTARD SEEDS
black also known as brown mustard seeds; more pungent than the white variety.
white also known as yellow mustard seeds; used ground for mustard powder and in most prepared mustards.

OSSO BUCCO another name used by butchers for veal shin, usually cut into 3cm- to 5cm-thick slices and used in the slow-cooked casserole of the same name.

PANCETTA an Italian unsmoked bacon; pork belly is cured in salt and spices then rolled into a sausage shape and dried for several weeks.

PAPRIKA ground dried sweet red capsicum (bell pepper); many grades and types are available, including sweet, hot, mild and smoked.

PINE NUTS also known as pignoli; not a nut but a small, cream-coloured kernel from pine cones. Best roasted before use to bring out the flavour.

POLENTA also known as cornmeal; a flour-like cereal made of dried corn (maize). Also the dish made from it.

PRESERVED LEMON whole or quartered salted lemons preserved in a mixture of water, or olive oil, and lemon juice. Occasionally spices such as cinnamon, clove and coriander are added. Available from delicatessens and specialty food shops. Use the rind only and rinse well before using.

RAISINS dried sweet grapes (traditionally muscatel grapes).

RED CURRY PASTE probably the most popular thai curry paste; a hot blend of different flavours that complements the richness of pork, duck and seafood, also works well in marinades and sauces.

RICE

arborio small, round-grain rice well-suited to absorb a large amount of liquid; the high level of starch makes it especially suitable for risottos, giving the dish its classic creaminess.

basmati a white, fragrant long-grained rice; the grains fluff up beautifully when cooked. It should be washed several times before cooking.

jasmine or thai jasmine, is a long-grained white rice recognised around the world for its perfumed aromatic quality, moist texture and the fact that it clings together after cooking. Jasmine rice is sometimes substituted for basmati rice.

ROCKET also called arugula, rugula and rucola; peppery green leaf eaten raw in salads or used in cooking. Baby rocket is smaller and less peppery.

ROLLED OATS flattened oat grain rolled into flakes and traditionally used for porridge. Instant oats are also available for a speedy breakfast, but use traditional oats for baking.

SHALLOTS also called french shallots, golden shallots or eschalots. Small and elongated, with a brown skin, they grow in tight clusters similar to garlic.

SILVER BEET also known as swiss chard and, incorrectly, spinach; has fleshy stalks and large leaves, both of which can be prepared as for spinach.

SMOKED HADDOCK smoked fish that has a white flesh and a milky smoky flavour; the skin is orange coloured.

SNOW PEA SPROUTS shoots of the snow pea (mange tout) plant. Available from supermarkets or greengrocers.

SOY SAUCE also known as sieu; made from fermented soya beans. Several types are available in supermarkets and Asian food stores. We use japanese soy sauce in our recipes unless otherwise indicated.

dark soy deep brown, almost black in colour; rich, with a thicker consistency than other types. Pungent, though not particularly salty, it is good for marinating.

japanese soy an all-purpose low-sodium soy sauce made with more wheat content than its Chinese counterparts; fermented in barrels and aged. Possibly the best table soy and the one to choose if you only want one variety.

light soy a fairly thin, pale but salty tasting sauce; used in dishes in which the natural colour of the ingredients is to be maintained. Not to be confused with salt-reduced or low-sodium soy sauces.

SPECK smoked pork.

SPINACH also known as english spinach and, incorrectly, silver beet. Baby spinach leaves are best eaten raw in salads; the larger leaves should be added last to soups, stews and stir-fries, and should be cooked until barely wilted.

TACO SEASONING MIX a packaged seasoning meant to duplicate the mild Mexican sauce made from oregano, cumin, chillies and other spices.

TOMATOES

bottled tomato pasta sauce a prepared tomato-based sauce (sometimes called ragu or sugo on the label); comes in varying degrees of thickness and levels of spicing.

canned whole peeled tomatoes in natural juices; available crushed, chopped or diced. Use undrained.

cherry also known as tiny tim or tom thumb tomatoes; a small, round tomato.

egg also called plum or roma, these are smallish, oval-shaped tomatoes much used in Italian cooking or salads.

paste triple-concentrated tomato puree.

puree canned pureed tomatoes (not tomato paste); substitute with fresh peeled and pureed tomatoes.

sauce also known as ketchup or catsup; a flavoured condiment made from tomatoes, vinegar and spices.

semi-dried partially dried tomato pieces in olive oil; softer and juicier than sun-dried, these are not a preserve therefore do not keep as long as sun-dried.

sun-dried tomato pieces that have been dried with salt; this dehydrates the tomato and concentrates the flavour. We generally use sun-dried tomatoes packaged in oil, unless otherwise specified.

truss small vine-ripened tomatoes with vine still attached.

TORTILLA thin, round unleavened bread originating in Mexico; available frozen, fresh or vacuum-packed. Two kinds of tortilla are available, one made from wheat flour and the other from corn.

TURMERIC also called kamin; is a rhizome related to galangal and ginger. Must be grated or pounded to release its acrid aroma and pungent flavour; known for the golden colour it imparts. Ground turmeric can be substituted for the less common fresh turmeric (use 2 teaspoons of ground turmeric plus a teaspoon of sugar for every 20g of fresh turmeric called for in a recipe).

WORCESTERSHIRE SAUCE a dark coloured thin condiment made from garlic, soy sauce, tamarind, onions, molasses, lime, anchovies, vinegar and seasonings. Available in supermarkets.

ZUCCHINI also known as courgette; small, pale- or dark-green, yellow or white vegetable belonging to the squash family. Harvested when young, its edible flowers can be stuffed with a mild cheese then deep-fried or oven-baked to make a delicious appetiser.

conversion chart

MEASURES

One Australian metric measuring cup holds approximately 250ml; one Australian metric tablespoon holds 20ml; one Australian metric teaspoon holds 5ml.

The difference between one country's measuring cups and another's is within a two- or three-teaspoon variance, and will not affect your cooking results. North America, New Zealand and the United Kingdom use a 15ml tablespoon.

All cup and spoon measurements are level. The most accurate way of measuring dry ingredients is to weigh them. When measuring liquids, use a clear glass or plastic jug with the metric markings.

We use large eggs with an average weight of 60g.

DRY MEASURES

METRIC	IMPERIAL
15g	½oz
30g	1oz
60g	2oz
90g	3oz
125g	4oz (¼lb)
155g	5oz
185g	6oz
220g	7oz
250g	8oz (½lb)
280g	9oz
315g	10oz
345g	11oz
375g	12oz (¾lb)
410g	13oz
440g	14oz
470g	15oz
500g	16oz (1lb)
750g	24oz (1½lb)
1kg	32oz (2lb)

LIQUID MEASURES

METRIC	IMPERIAL
30ml	1 fluid oz
60ml	2 fluid oz
100ml	3 fluid oz
125ml	4 fluid oz
150ml	5 fluid oz
190ml	6 fluid oz
250ml	8 fluid oz
300ml	10 fluid oz
500ml	16 fluid oz
600ml	20 fluid oz
1000ml (1 litre)	1¾ pints

LENGTH MEASURES

METRIC	IMPERIAL
3mm	⅛in
6mm	¼in
1cm	½in
2cm	¾in
2.5cm	1in
5cm	2in
6cm	2½in
8cm	3in
10cm	4in
13cm	5in
15cm	6in
18cm	7in
20cm	8in
22cm	9in
25cm	10in
28cm	11in
30cm	12in (1ft)

OVEN TEMPERATURES

The oven temperatures in this book are for conventional ovens; if you have a fan-forced oven, decrease the temperature by 10-20 degrees.

	°C (CELSIUS)	°F (FAHRENHEIT)
Very slow	120	250
Slow	150	300
Moderately slow	160	325
Moderate	180	350
Moderately hot	200	400
Hot	220	425
Very hot	240	475

The imperial measurements used in these recipes are approximate only. Measurements for cake pans are approximate only. Using same-shaped cake pans of a similar size should not affect the outcome of your baking. We measure the inside top of the cake pan to determine sizes.

index

A

asparagus
    asparagus, egg and bacon bake 14
    tuna and asparagus crumble 57

B

bacon
    asparagus, egg and bacon bake 14
    carbonara gnocchi bake 6
    cheesy chicken, tomato and
        bacon rigatoni 81
    creamy chicken, bacon and
        corn chowder 89
    egg and bacon pie 112
    mashed potato and bacon bake 48
    potato, bacon and blue cheese
        bake 45
baked meatballs 102
beef
    baked meatballs 102
    beef ragu cannelloni 114
    creamy bolognese pasta bake 22
    pastitsio 18
    stew with chive dumplings 101
    sweet and sour meatballs 117
    tomato, beef and pea lasagne 12
biryani, chicken, with cauliflower
    and peas 90
broccoli and cheese penne with
    garlic and lemon crumbs 17

C

carbonara gnocchi bake 6
cassoulet
    chicken, sausage and bean 77
    pork sausage 110
cauliflower and broccoli gratin 38
cheese
    broccoli and cheese penne with
        garlic and lemon crumbs 17
    cheese and vegetable polenta
        bake 33
    cheesy chicken, tomato and
        bacon rigatoni 81
    classic macaroni cheese 20
    fetta crust 118
    gremolata and parmesan topping 78
    potato, bacon and blue cheese
        bake 45
    prawns and fetta with crispy fillo 62
    pumpkin, pea and fetta risotto 37
    three-cheese sauce 46
    topping 18
chicken
    biryani with cauliflower and peas 90
    cheesy chicken, tomato and bacon
        rigatoni 81
    chicken and eggplant parmigiana 74
    chicken and sweet corn bake 80
    chicken cacciatore with gremolata
        and parmesan topping 78
    chicken, sausage and bean
        cassoulet 77
    chicken stroganoff with potato
        topping 93
    chicken, zucchini and mushroom
        lasagne 87
    creamy chicken, bacon and
        corn chowder 89
    mexican chicken tortilla bake 83
    red curry chicken risotto 88
    red wine and rosemary chicken
        with polenta crust 94
    spicy chicken and ratatouille pilaf 84
chive dumplings 34, 101
chorizo and chickpea stew 113
classic macaroni cheese 20
creamed spinach 98
creamy bolognese pasta bake 22
creamy chicken, bacon and
    corn chowder 89
crumble oat topping 57
crust
    fetta 118
    polenta 94, 105
curried lentil pies 29

D

dumplings
    chive 34, 101
    parsley 109

E

egg and bacon pie 112
eggplant parmigiana 30

F

fennel and leek gratin 39
fetta crust 118
frittata
    potato 49
    rocket pesto and spaghetti 9

G

gnocchi
    carbonara gnocchi bake 6
    spinach and kumara 26
goulash, veal, with parsley dumplings 109
gremolata and parmesan topping 78

H

ham, potato, leek and artichoke bake 51

J

jansson's temptation 59

L

lamb
    lamb and eggplant pot pies with
        fetta crust 118
    lamb shank shepherd's pie 98
lasagne
    chicken, zucchini and mushroom 87
    mexican chicken tortilla bake 83
    salmon and zucchini 54
    seafood mornay 8
    tomato, beef and pea 12
leek
    fennel and leek gratin 39
    ham, potato, leek and artichoke
        bake 51

M

macaroni cheese, classic 20
meatballs
    baked 102
    sweet and sour 117
mexican chicken tortilla bake 83

O

osso bucco with polenta crust 105

P

parmigiana
    chicken and eggplant 74
    eggplant 30
parsley dumplings 109
pasta
    asparagus, egg and bacon bake 14
    beef ragu cannelloni 114
    broccoli and cheese penne with
      garlic and lemon crumbs 17
    carbonara gnocchi bake 6
    cheesy chicken, tomato and
      bacon rigatoni 81
    classic macaroni cheese 20
    creamy bolognese pasta bake 22
    pastitsio 18
    penne arrabbiata bake 11
    pumpkin, spinach and ricotta
      cannelloni 15
    rocket pesto and spaghetti frittata 9
    salami antipasto pasta 106
    seafood mornay lasagnes 8
    spaghetti rosa bake 10
    spicy sardine and spaghetti bake 61
    spicy tuna pasta bake 67
    spinach and ricotta pasta slice 16
    tuna mornay with pasta 21
pastitsio 18
penne arrabbiata bake 11
pies
    curried lentil 29
    egg and bacon 112
    lamb and eggplant pot pies with
      fetta crust 118
    lamb shank shepherd's pie 98
    salmon, silver beet and rice 70
pilaf, spicy chicken and ratatouille
    pilaf 84
polenta crust 94, 105
pork sausage cassoulet 110
potato
    creamy fish and potato bake 60
    frittata 49

gnocchi with three-cheese sauce 46
gratin with caramelised onion 42
ham, potato, leek and artichoke
    bake 51
jansson's temptation 59
lemon and tomato, with 44
mashed potato and bacon bake 48
potato, bacon and blue cheese
    bake 45
salmon, potato and rocket cake 58
sardine, potato and lemon bake 68
smoked haddock potato bake 65
twice-baked 50
prawns and fetta with crispy fillo 62
pumpkin, pea and fetta risotto 37
pumpkin, spinach and ricotta
    cannelloni 15

R

red curry chicken risotto 88
risotto
    pumpkin, pea and fetta 37
    red curry chicken 88
    sausage 121
rocket pesto and spaghetti frittata 9
root vegetable gratin 32

S

salami antipasto pasta 106
salmon
    salmon and zucchini lasagne 54
    salmon bread and butter pudding 66
    salmon, potato and rocket cake 58
    salmon, silver beet and rice pie 70
sardine, potato and lemon bake 68
sauce
    sweet and sour 117
    tomato basil 26
    white 87
sausage risotto 121
seafood
    creamy fish and potato bake 60
    jansson's temptation 59
    prawns and fetta with crispy fillo 62
    salmon and zucchini lasagne 54
    salmon bread and butter pudding 66
    salmon, potato and rocket cake 58
    salmon, silver beet and rice pie 70

sardine, potato and lemon bake 68
seafood mornay lasagnes 8
smoked haddock potato bake 65
spicy sardine and spaghetti bake 61
spicy tuna pasta bake 67
tuna and asparagus crumble 57
tuna and corn bake 69
tuna mornay with pasta 21
smoked haddock potato bake 65
spaghetti rosa bake 10
spicy chicken and ratatouille pilaf 84
spicy sardine and spaghetti bake 61
spicy tuna pasta bake 67
spinach and kumara gnocchi 26
spinach and ricotta pasta slice 16
spinach, creamed 98
stew
    beef, with chive dumplings 101
    chorizo and chickpea 113
stroganoff, chicken with
    potato topping 93
sweet and sour meatballs 117
sweet and sour sauce 117

T

three-cheese sauce 46
tomato basil sauce 26
tomato, beef and pea lasagne 12
tuna
    tuna and asparagus crumble 57
    tuna and corn bake 69
    tuna mornay with pasta 21
twice-baked potatoes 50

V

veal
    goulash with parsley dumplings 109
    osso bucco with polenta crust 105
vegie casserole with chive dumplings 34
vegetable gratin, root 32
vegetable and cheese polenta bake 33

W

white sauce 87

Published in 2011 by ACP Books, Sydney

ACP Books are published by ACP Magazines
a division of Nine Entertainment Co.

ACP BOOKS

General manager Christine Whiston
Associate publisher Seymour Cohen
Editor-in-chief Susan Tomnay
Creative director & designer Hieu Chi Nguyen
Junior designer Josh Yarbrough
Senior editor Kirsty McKenzie
Food director Pamela Clark
Food editor Rebecca Squadrito
Sales & rights director Brian Cearnes
Marketing manager Bridget Cody
Senior business analyst Rebecca Varela
Operations manager David Scotto
Production manager Victoria Jefferys
Circulation manager Sarah Lloyd
Circulation analyst Nicole Pearson

Published by ACP Books, a division of
ACP Magazines Ltd, 54 Park St, Sydney;
GPO Box 4088, Sydney, NSW 2001.
phone (02) 9282 8618; fax (02) 9267 9438.

acpbooks@acpmagazines.com.au;
www.acpbooks.com.au

Printed by C&C Offset Printing, China.

Australia Distributed by Network Services,
phone +61 2 9282 8777; fax +61 2 9264 3278;
networkweb@networkservicescompany.com.au
New Zealand Distributed by Netlink Distribution Company,
phone (9) 366 9966; ask@ndc.co.nz
South Africa Distributed by PSD Promotions,
phone (27 11) 392 6065/6/7; fax (27 11) 392 6079/80; orders@psdprom.co.za

Gratins & bakes / [food director Pamela Clark].
ISBN: 978 174245 136 7 (pbk.)
Notes: Includes index.
Subjects: Baking. Casserole cooking.
Other Authors/Contributors: Clark, Pamela.
Also Titled: Australian women's weekly.
Dewey Number: 641.71

© ACP Magazines Ltd 2011
ABN 18 053 273 546
This publication is copyright. No part of it may be reproduced or transmitted in any form without the written permission of the publishers.

Recipe development Nicole Dicker, Sharon Kennedy, Lucy Nunes, Rebecca Squadrito
Nutritional information Rebecca Squadrito

Photographer Julie Crespel
Stylist Kate Brown
Food preparation Emma McCaskill
Cover front Classic macaroni cheese, page 20
Cover back Carbonara gnocchi bake, page 6

To order books
phone 136 116 (within Australia) or
order online at www.acpbooks.com.au
Send recipe enquiries to:
recipeenquiries@acpmagazines.com.au